D0479429

ALSO BY KATHRYN BERLA

Dream Me
The House at 758
The Kitty Committee (2018)

GOING PLACES

Kathryn Berla
Amberjack Publishing
New York | Idaho

AMBERJACK
P U B L I S H I N G

Amberjack Publishing
1472 E. Iron Eagle Dr.
Eagle, Idaho 83616
http://amberjackpublishing.com

Publisher's Cataloging-in-Publication data
Names: Berla, Kathryn, author.
Title: Going places / by Kathryn Berla.
Description: New York, NY; Eagle, ID: Amberjack Publishing, 2018.
Identifiers: ISBN 978-1-944995-53-9 (pbk.) | 978-1-944995-54-6 (ebook) | LCCN 2017946718
Subjects: LCSH Interpersonal relations--Fiction. | Friendship--Fiction. | Artists--Fiction. | Dementia--Fiction. | Dog-walking--Fiction. | Coming of age--Fiction. | Bildungsromans. | BISAC YOUNG ADULT FICTION / General
Classification: LCC PZ7.B45323 Go 2018 | DDC [Fic]—dc23

Cover Design: Maddie Ceglecki

I READ IT OVER ONE LAST TIME.

Did I argue my point effectively? After two weeks of planning was I overthinking the whole thing? It was already the first of August, and sleeping in until noon was almost a thing of the past. The first day of school loomed like the grim reaper. I clicked SEND before time ran out and Mom's lunch break was over. Before time ran out and my summer vacation was over. Then I sat back and held my breath. Not literally, of course, even though it felt like it.

To: BigWheel@home.com
From: MomWheel@home.com
Subject: Proposal

We need to talk. I was going to say something last night but decided it's better to lay it all out for you first. I have a proposal that you probably won't like, but please read this whole email before you answer.

I think I should be homeschooled this year.

These are my reasons:

(1) I only need two classes to graduate, and I've proved I work better on my own.

(2) Senior year of high school is a complete waste of time. Nobody pays attention, and half the kids don't bother showing up for class half the time.

(3) College isn't a requirement for becoming a graphic novelist, and there's no doubt in my mind now that's what I want to do when I graduate.

(4) Quentin Tarantino (famous film director) dropped out of school at the age of 15 and his mother didn't care, and look where he is now.

(5) I've done ALL the research. I downloaded ALL the paperwork. The only thing I need is your signature in a few places. I PROMISE I'll take care of EVERYTHING!!! I'm begging you to say YES!!!!

-Hudson

P.S. I've been thinking about this all summer so don't think it's something I just came up with.

P.P.S. And please don't think this has anything to do with a failure on your part about being a good mother, etc.

It wasn't that I was scared of Mom, who is actually a really nice and understanding person. It's just that I was scared she'd say "no," and over the past few weeks I'd managed to convince myself this was the only possible way of surviving my senior year of high school. I wasn't prepared to deal with a flat-out *No*. Couldn't even consider that awful possibility. What I *was* prepared for was a major battle that I planned on winning before the homeschool program registration deadline. So I sat in the kitchen staring at the computer screen, waiting for Mom to return fire. I checked my inbox. One new message. *Top Trending Tweets*. And then the dinosaur desktop froze. Instead of bolting for the laptop in my bedroom, I forced myself to take a deep breath and calmly reboot. In order to prevail against Mom, it was important to stay focused and maintain my composure. I leaned back in my chair while the computer clucked and the screen changed from white to blue to black to white again.

The kitchen. A huge part of my life had played out there. Mom hated it because she didn't have the money to update it. She claimed it taunted her every day of her life. Puke-yellow Formica counters; the rust countertop footprint of a can of baked beans; the floor that was supposed to look like a tile floor but was really just a sheet of vinyl curling up at the corners; the cabinets that never closed all the way; fluorescent lights that buzzed, flickered, and hummed like crazy; and the refrigerator hummed too. And rocked like it was about to fall on top of you whenever you opened it.

Taped to the refrigerator was a note. The one my fifth grade teacher sent to my parents. The one Mom refused to let me take down even after all this time.

The one that taunted me every day the same way the kitchen taunted her.

> *Dear Mr. and Mrs. Wheeler,*
>
> *It isn't every day I'm motivated to write a letter like this, so I want the two of you to know just how meaningful this is. Hudson is one of those students who comes along very rarely, so I consider myself blessed to have had him in my class this year. When it comes to good citizenry, he has no peer, always ready to lend a helping hand. Hudson is extremely well-liked by both faculty and the student body. He is motivated, helpful, thinks creatively and unselfishly. You've succeeded admirably in your job of parenting to have produced such a fine young man. It's obvious to me that Hudson is going places!*
>
> *D. Thompson*

I memorized the letter, that's how many times I've read it. Every time I opened the refrigerator in the last eight years looking for something to eat (at least ten times a day), there it was. Technically it should have been addressed to Major and Mrs. Wheeler because that's what Dad was, a Major in the army. But he never saw the letter. A month after Mrs. Thompson mailed it to my house, my dad was killed in Iraq. I was the student body president that year and believed what Mrs. Thompson said. I wasn't sure exactly where I was going, but I knew it would be somewhere big. Somewhere that would make me happy and make my parents proud, and I didn't mean just middle school.

But after Dad died, we went through our sad years where I sometimes had to act more grown-up than I was just to help Mom get through the day. After that, where I was going didn't seem so important anymore. We got through the sadness, of course. But the letter that used to feel like a promise began to feel like a dare. And there I was trying to disappear from school altogether. What would Mrs. Thompson think if she knew what I was doing?

The computer clucked a few more times while it finished updating. Finally, it was ready to go, and I breathed deeply as I signed back into my email account. One new message. Mom. I imagined her tapping out the response in that clumsy one-fingered way she did on the phone. Probably hyperventilating all the while. She'd put herself through nursing school and wouldn't be able to understand why anyone would turn their back on the luxury of being educated without having to work. To her, school wasn't just important, it was everything.

Is this about Cameron? she wrote.

I replied, *WHAT??? of course not!!!!* Okay, it wasn't just about Cameron, it was about Griffin too. My two best friends since grade school until last year when Griffin transferred to the school across town after his family bought a new house. And then to make matters worse, Cameron fell into a ridiculously serious relationship with a girl I didn't even like.

When you grow up as a threesome so close you're almost brothers, there's a co-dependency that's hard to see your way out of. I couldn't wish Griffin back into his old house, and wishing for Cameron to break up with his girlfriend only made me feel evil, which I probably was.

But if I admitted all of that to Mom, she'd go on a whole rant about making new friends and joining clubs to meet new people. All the stuff that sounds so great to parents when they're lecturing you. The reality is something else. Something parents just don't get. You can't reinvent yourself when you're a senior in high school. Everyone knows that.

I was so done with school and couldn't see its relevancy to my life anymore. Homeschooling would be cool. I hadn't really thought out what I'd do with all my free time while Mom was at work, but I did have a pile of graphic novels to get through, and I wanted to write and illustrate one of my own. So maybe Mom didn't exactly like the idea of me lying around all day reading my "comic books," as she called them, much to my annoyance.

Well I think it is, she wrote back. *But in any case, the way I see it is we both have our jobs. Mine is being a nurse. Yours is being a student.*

She tried to reason with me, but for every point she made, I already had three counter-points ready to lob back at her. After the first week, she realized I was serious. After the second week, she actually started listening to me. After the third week (just in time, because school was about to start) she finally surrendered. I was nothing if not persuasive when it came to Mom. I sometimes still caught her staring at the letter on the refrigerator that promised I was "going places," and maybe she really believed it. But it wasn't total surrender. She had her conditions, so we drew up a contract which we both signed.

> *Hudson Wheeler promises to take the following classes at La Costa High during this upcoming school year:*
>
> *AP Art*
>
> *Physical Education*
>
> *He also promises to apply to two (2) colleges for which he has a reasonable chance of being accepted.*
>
> *From this day forward he will pay rent on the first of the month in the amount of $200.*
>
> *Signed:*
>
> *Deborah Wheeler , Hudson Wheeler*

The art class was required due to the fact that my mother was worried about me having zero social interaction with my peers. Taking a class in something I loved and was good at, she thought would go down easier. She probably also secretly hoped it would help to increase my self-esteem which was something she worried about a lot.

P.E. was required because she didn't want me to

turn into a couch potato. Her philosophy was that everyone needed to get out and do something active for at least an hour each day. But since P.E. was an elective for seniors, I had a lot of choices. I chose yoga, the main reason being the favorable female-to-male ratio. This would ensure two things: 1. No competition against guys in a physical way. That never worked out very well for me in the past. 2. I still had a wild hope of doing something (anything) with a girl (any girl) before graduating from high school.

The two college applications and the rent . . . that was Mom hoping I'd come to my senses before it was too late.

I wasn't that same kid who inspired Mrs. Thompson to write the refrigerator note all those years ago. Fate had played a couple of dirty tricks on me over the years. But in the beginning of my final year of high school, I had a renewed sense of hope-fulness. I felt light. Free. As I roamed the hallways of school on my first day, I felt like an adult in a sea of children. I could leave and go home in just a few hours. And I felt something else I hadn't felt in a long time. Excitement about my future.

>>>

The first day of school arrived without the usual pit in my stomach. Only two classes meant I'd be in and out in less than two hours. I could actually wait to eat breakfast until after getting home.

Nothing was going to ruin the high I had walking

into yoga class. Except maybe Gus Ligety. There he was, posed on his yoga mat like Buddha, surrounded by girls. Girls. Girls. And more girls. Girls dressed in skintight outfits—some of them really revealing. Sleepy-eyed girls. Sleek-haired girls. An ocean of girls. I tried my best to block out Gus and the two other guys in the room. They weren't exactly chick-magnet types of guys, but then neither was I. The guys those girls really wanted to be with wouldn't be caught dead in a yoga class. Later in the year, those same guys would make a point to stop and stare into our classroom, pointing and laughing at us (me and Gus) until the teacher turned around and shooed them away with a dirty look.

When I arrived (late) to class, everyone was already lotus-style on three neatly spaced rows of yoga mats. I realized two things: 1. As an unfairly vertically-challenged male, being barefoot in class did nothing to disguise my short stature. "Unfairly," I say, because my father was tall. But my mom's short, and at seventeen I was taking after her in that depart-ment. 2. The loose basketball shorts I had on weren't going to cut it in yoga class. Even Gus knew that. He was decked out in what I assumed were men's yoga pants—at least they were long and didn't slide away to reveal everything no guy wants to show at school. I did some fast thinking and made a decision to take my place all the way in the back, hidden behind two rows of girls from the teacher's forward facing view.

"Hud-man!" Gus called out, prompting a harsh

look from Ms. Senger, our youngish and semi-hot instructor. "What's up, bro? Come sit over here with me. We dudes have to stick together."

Ms. Senger brought a slender finger up to her pursed lips.

"Mr . . .?"

"Wheeler." Why was I stupidly late on my first day? I was breaking my own rule of blending into the background. I'd known since middle school that you don't call attention to yourself by walking into a class-room late.

"Mr. Wheeler, please find a space. There are mats in the back."

I unrolled a mat and inserted myself between two girls who giggled while they moved aside to let me squeeze in.

Once seated, I could check out everyone else from the safe vantage point of the back of the room. It was a beginner's class so I assumed everyone was going to be as bad as me, but I knew the girls had an advantage when it came to flexibility. Gus, I knew, unfortunately since preschool. He seemed to have a magic mirror that gave him confidence beyond anything he deserved. He was annoying but basically a nice guy in very small doses.

Directly to my left was a girl I knew by the name of Alana Love. She showed up in my Art History class late in our junior year with her messy dirty-blonde hair that looked like it'd never met a brush. Not in a bad way, don't get me wrong. Definitely sexy.

She also had big, expressive puppy eyes. Or maybe they were kitten eyes. The rest of her face—some of it worked, and some of it didn't. Her nose was a little crooked, her lips were a little thin, and she had a couple of zits on her chin. She also had a tattoo on one side of her neck: a flowering vine of purples and pinks. The first time I saw it I actually thought it was a bruise, like someone had tried to strangle her. Over time, I came to admire it, and my own bare neck seemed naked in comparison. Other kids at school had tattoos but none as out-there as Alana's.

Sitting next to her, I could smell Alana, and she smelled really nice. All in all, she was the kind of girl you could fantasize about, even though for me that was just about any girl with most body parts intact. A girl named Penelope was on my other side. In different circumstances, she might have been the object of my desire, but with Alana Love so close, Penelope didn't stand a chance.

Ms. Senger led us through the Sukhasana, the cat-cow pose, the tree pose, and some others I don't remember. By the time we were through I was really feeling it. And it didn't help that I had to constantly pull my shorts down over my knees. Gus groaned loudly, but I tried to suck it up for the benefit of Alana Love, not wanting her to think I was one of *those* guys. Inflexible. Looking for an easy A or an easy girl. I wanted her to respect me, so I threw myself into every pose and promised myself the next day would be easier. I'd stretch before class and wear sweat pants instead of shorts. Were our seating assignments permanent? I hoped so.

TWENTY MINUTES IS A LONG TIME...

. . . between classes if you think about how much stuff happens in the regular passing period, which is only five minutes. Entire lives change during passing period. Relationships begin. People get dumped. Weekend parties are planned. With the extra fifteen minutes between zero and first period, I'd already changed out of my yoga clothes and was walking to art class while most of the seniors were still cruising the senior lot looking for a place to park.

"Wait up, Hud-man!" Gus jogged up from behind just as I was closing the gap between myself and Alana, who was about ten paces ahead.

"Do me a favor, Gus," I began. Was I being a jerk because of my empty stomach? Or the fact that Gus just ruined my next move with Alana (which wasn't exactly planned out to be honest)? "Don't call me

13

Hud-man and I won't call you . . ."

"Call me what?"

"Gus-man."

"No problem."

We walked in silence long enough for Gus to notice Alana in front of us. He nudged me in the ribs with his elbow, which succeeded in making me even crankier.

"You going to hit that?" he asked way too loudly.

"Hit what?" The hungry pit in my stomach turned to nausea.

"You know." He nudged me again and I pushed his arm away. "*That*." He motioned with his chin towards Alana who was possibly within hearing distance. At that moment, I was grateful the human ear points forward, not back.

"No, I'm not going to *hit* that," I whispered hoarsely.

"Mind if I do?"

He didn't wait for my answer. "How'd you like yoga today?" he bellowed at Alana's back. The vine on the side of her neck twisted as she turned to look behind her. "Bet you're feeling pretty sore."

"Oh hey," she said. I desperately wanted to protect her from his lunacy without identifying myself as his friend but saw no way out. "It was fun," she smiled. "Easy. I've been doing yoga since I was ten."

"I thought this was a beginner's class, didn't you, Hud-man . . ." he trailed off, warned by the fierce look in my eye. "Hud?"

"It fits with my schedule," she said. "I talked to Miss Senger before class, and she said I could go at my own pace. Your name's Hud?" She instinctively reacted the same way most people do when faced with a conversation with Gus. Change the subject and pivot away from him as quickly as possible. I felt a sudden wave of sympathy. It couldn't be easy being Gus, no matter how much confidence he dripped.

"Hudson, actually."

"You were in my Art History last year."

"Yeah. You came at the end."

"My father has a wacky job. We move around a lot."

"Wacky?" Gus reinserted himself into the conversation. "What does he do?"

"Auditing for a bunch of big companies."

Neither one of us knew what that meant, so we scrambled for a follow-up. Conversation would have been easier without Gus breathing down my neck, but to be fair, he probably felt the same way. Maybe I *should* have claimed Alana when he asked me. Should have told him I was going to "hit that." I just couldn't imagine those words coming out of my mouth.

"Heard you're homeschooling this year." How is it that Gus always knew everything about everyone? "Did you suddenly get religious or spend time in the slammer over the summer?" He laughed hard at that and then turned to Alana whose blank face demanded an explanation. "The only people who homeschool are religious kids and incorrigibles."

Alana beamed her saucer eyes on me. "If you're homeschooling, why are you here?"

"I'm only taking two classes. I leave after art . . . next period."

"AP Art?"

"Yup."

"I guess we're in the same class again."

"So why are you homeschooling?" Gus insisted.

"Senior year's a waste of time. I'm trying to start a few businesses and need time to work on my novel."

I didn't feel the need to mention college was not in my future. I also wished for a trapdoor to suddenly open and swallow up Gus.

"Novel?" Alana's wide eyes opened wider than I thought possible. "You're writing a novel?"

"A graphic novel."

I wasn't exactly writing one but was sure thinking about it, and I had been ever since I'd discovered the genre and been swept up in it. There'd been some false starts and stops, but they hadn't led to much.

"I'd love to see it sometime. What's it about?"

"What kind of businesses are you starting?" Gus interrupted, and I was grateful I didn't have to explain the graphic novel that didn't yet exist.

"I have two." This was true. I'd gotten the idea for my dog-walking business after listening to my neighbor's dog bark all summer long. I had three clients. My neighbor's one-eyed Chihuahua, driven to near-psychosis by long, endless days of boredom. A three-legged Labrador whose owner had emphysema.

And a snow-white, perfectly-coiffed poodle that wanted nothing more than to go outside, but lacked the delivery system to get him there until I came along. I'd printed some cards and knocked on doors of houses where I'd seen or heard dogs before. "One's a dog-walking business."

"Dog walking?" Gus guffawed. "Give me a break. Your mom lets you be homeschooled so you can walk dogs? Dude, you must have her twisted around your little finger. What a scam!"

"What's your other business?" Alana asked.

This one was tricky, but I was proud of the idea even though I only had one client. It seemed to me like an easy way to sit back and collect money with little or no expended effort, not that walking dogs took much. "You know those commercials on TV where an old person falls down and calls for help by pushing a button they wear around their neck?"

"You're the guy who runs over to their house to pick them up after they fall down?"

If there was any doubt, I knew then that Gus was determined to make me look bad in front of Alana. It was all part of the "guys trying to impress girls" thing. If we were reindeer, we'd be butting horns. If we were beta fish we'd be fanning our fins at each other. But we were just two awkward guys trying to outwit each other. Or at least Gus was trying to outwit me, and I was trying to out-class him.

"So I started thinking," I talked right over him, doing my best to ignore his last dig. "There are probably a lot of old people living by themselves who have problems that aren't exactly emergencies but fall just under the level of emergency."

"Yeah," Alana stopped outside our classroom. This would be where I hoped to get rid of Gus. "I'll bet there are. So what exactly would you do?"

She didn't go inside so we all just stood there. Five minutes before class started.

"I give them a prepaid cell phone and program it with my direct number. Then they can call me anytime if they need me for an emergency right below the level of a 911 call."

"*Hah!*" Gus snorted. I purposely avoided looking at him.

"Cool." Alana smiled, and a tiny dimple formed in the middle of her chin. Right in between two of her three zits. I'd never noticed it before, probably because I'd never been that close. "Like, what would that be?"

I truthfully didn't know, and, actually, I was hoping there wasn't such a thing as an emergency right below the level of a 911 call. My plan was to charge a monthly rate and not have to do any work.

"Wow. So much stuff," I said as seriously and mysteriously as possible.

Alana looked a little skeptical. "How many customers do you have?"

I looked down at the ground, wishing lying came more easily to me. "So far I only have one," I said. "But my mom's a nurse, and she has some leads. There're a lot of upsides to the business since my costs don't increase much as new business comes in. Same with the dog-walking."

"But you can only walk so many dogs at one time," Gus challenged.

"I can take different group of dogs out at different times if more business comes in."

Gus's mouth opened then closed silently like a fish. I'd finally succeeded in silencing him.

"I love dogs," Alana said. "But I never got to have one since we moved around so much."

"Maybe you can come with me to walk the dogs sometime." It came out before I could stop myself. *Idiot!* And with Gus right there as an eyewitness . . . "If you want," I added foolishly, like she didn't know she had a choice in the matter.

"Yeah, maybe," she said. "Bell's about to ring. You going in?"

There were four chairs to a table, and I spotted two empty seats side by side. I moved quickly to claim them, assuming Alana was right behind me, and set my backpack down before noticing she was already across the room sliding into another chair obviously reserved for her by the looks of the jacket hanging over the back. And the guy next to her . . . I knew who he was. A nice enough guy. Decent artist. Okay-looking if you like that clean-cut, athletic kind of look. Tall. Bryce Something. Not the kind of guy I'd picture with Alana, but then again, neither was I. All right, maybe she had a boyfriend, and that wasn't the worst thing in the world. There were still nineteen other girls in yoga class, including Penelope. There was still a whole school year in front of me. Or was Bryce Something maybe just a friend?

Alana glanced across the room and gave me one of those four finger fluttering type of waves. The kind that little kids use. And old ladies. And pretty girls.

>>>

THINGS TO DO TODAY:

1. Start art project
2. Walk dogs
3. Work on graphic novel for real
4. Do a little homeschool homework every day so I don't have to cram for bi-monthly meetings
5. Empty dishwasher and wash dishes

The cell phone ringing two inches from my right ear rattled me back to consciousness. How was it already noon? Caller ID showed Mrs. Dickinson, my one and only emergency contact client. I coughed a few times and cleared my throat to get the sleep out of my voice.

"Mrs. Dickinson, are you calling for help?"

"Why, yes dear. Is it okay to call now?"

"It's okay anytime you need me." This was my first ever call, so the adrenaline was pumping. I hadn't expected to get a call so soon, or actually even at all. Mom took the car to work which left me only with my bike, but Mrs. Dickinson was just four blocks down the street.

"I know you said I was only supposed to call for emergencies but . . ."

"No. Actually, for emergencies call 911. Call me for anything just less than an emergency."

How well could I market this business if my one and only client didn't even understand its purpose? But in fairness, neither did I.

"Well, that's what I meant. This isn't really an emergency, but it's just less than one. I need help with my email. I've tried and tried to get onto my account, but it keeps saying . . . wait a minute, I wrote it down . . . *invalid password*. I know I'm typing it correctly because it's my name."

"Mrs. Dickinson . . ." The clock on the wall showed twelve, and I still hadn't eaten breakfast. My stomach was growling, and nothing on my list had been checked off. The list I so optimistically created when I got home from school that morning. Was it only that morning? Alana? Gus? *That* morning?

"Mrs. Dickinson. Just give me twenty minutes and I'll be there."

"Please hurry," she said.

Mrs. Dickinson did have a dog that, as far as I knew, was never allowed further than her mailbox. A chubby but mellow cocker spaniel that would be a perfect addition to my existing team of three dogs. All I needed was to slowly work Mrs. Dickinson into the idea, convincing her the dog needed socializing and exercise.

"I'll be there in fifteen."

"Can you make it in ten?"

THE CUSTOMER IS ALWAYS RIGHT...

. . . but when they're not, you have to tell them they're wrong in a way that lets them think that they're right. If you can't, then just keep your mouth shut or risk losing your customer.

"It's a good thing I signed up for your service." Mrs. Dickinson smelled like lavender which made me think of the flowering vine on the side of Alana's neck. "I don't know what I would have done otherwise. Come with me, the computer's in my sewing room."

"No problem, Mrs. Dickinson. Technically . . ." I had to be careful here, and saying it to her back as I followed her down the dark and narrow hallway seemed like a less hostile way of setting her straight. Family pictures covered both walls. "My service is really for things that fall just below the level of an emergency."

"Like what?" She stopped suddenly and turned to face me.

"Like, uh . . ." Her liquid blue eyes filled with accusation. *Careful, Hudson.* "Like, for instance . . . say a stranger knocks on your door and you don't feel safe answering it. You could call me, and I could come by to make sure no one's hanging around, scoping out your house or something."

"Oh, dear," Mrs. Dickinson's face went white with fear. "I'd never thought of someone knocking on my door to case the place. Do you think that's what they're up to? A young man came by just last week wanting to know if I needed my gutters cleaned."

I didn't want to scare her, but I needed to set boundaries.

"I'm not saying that people who knock on your door are all bad. But if you feel nervous about anything." I tried to think of a less scary example of my services. "Let's say you go to get in your car and find the tank is empty. You could call me, and I could come by with a can of gas to get you to the nearest station."

That wasn't exactly what I was thinking when I came up with the idea for my business, but it was the first thing that came to mind.

"But I have AAA for that purpose."

This was wasn't going well.

"Or if you're feeling sick. Maybe you have the flu or something. I could go to the store and bring you medicine." That seemed easy enough, and people didn't usually get the flu more than once a year, if that.

"I suppose so." She flipped the light switch and the dark hallway lit up so I could clearly see the family photos. "But if my email isn't working I can't speak to my children and grandchildren," she motioned her hand towards the wall where children and grandchildren surrounded us. They smiled down at me like I was the only thing standing between Mrs. Dickinson and no email.

"You're right," I knew when I was beaten. "You're absolutely right. This is very important and qualifies as something . . . just below the level of an emergency."

She smiled, and I followed her into the sewing room.

"Now you take all the time you need while I go look for a phone number. A gentleman I met at the Senior Center is interested in your services. I told him all about you."

Two minutes later, I went out to look for Mrs. Dickinson and found her rummaging through a kitchen drawer.

"I know I put it here." I could hear the frustration in her voice. "Darn it." She looked up at me. "Did you fix my email?"

"Yes. The problem was you had your Caps Lock on, and your password is case sensitive. If it ever happens again just press the Caps Lock key again."

"Wait a minute." She pulled a sticky pad from the kitchen drawer and wrote in flowery cursive, her hand trembling ever so slightly.

If email password doesn't work, check Caps Lock button.

"I'll put this on my computer." She peeled the purple sticky note from its pad. "Now what was I doing here?"

"Looking for the phone number of the gentleman who wants my services?" I was proud of myself for remembering to say *gentleman* instead of *guy* or *man*.

"That's right. I don't know what I've done with it, but I'll keep looking. He's new at the Senior Center, so maybe I'll run into him there again if I can't find it."

"I appreciate it, Mrs. Dickinson." Lady, the cocker spaniel, was lying on a pillow in the corner of the kitchen. She lifted her head and thumped her tail against the pillow when she saw me. She seemed pretty lazy, but maybe she was just old.

"Hi, Lady girl!" I walked over and gave her a few friendly rubs behind the ears to get Mrs. Dickinson used to the idea that Lady and I were friends. I'd wait for the *gentleman's* phone number before I asked for Lady's business. "And Mrs. Dickinson? You should change your password. It's a bad idea to use your name."

"But it's so easy to remember." She looked as hurt as if I'd just slapped one of her grandchildren.

"That's exactly the point. If it's easy for you to remember, then it's easy for someone else to guess.

Someone who could possibly hack into your account."

"Oh dear."

There went the scared look again. I'd have to remember with Mrs. Dickinson it was a balancing act of getting her to do the right thing without destroying her peace of mind.

"It's okay for now. Let me know when you want to change it, and I'll come over and help you." I thought about the online tutorial I read about entrepreneurship . . . *always ask for the business.* "And please give me a call when you find the gentleman's number." I hoped the *when* as opposed to *if* would plant it more firmly in her mind. "Bye, Lady!"

Lady thumped her tail politely in response before collapsing once again into the soft pillow.

NO NEED TO JUDGE MYSELF SO HARSHLY . . .

. . . if all my goals weren't accomplished on the first day. Or so I told myself. After all, a list was only a suggestion. It might take a few weeks to get the hang of my new life as a self-directed homeschooled student running two businesses and writing the great American graphic novel.

In the meantime, I'd better pay special attention to the things Mom would notice when she came home. She was the one who held the key to my future, or at least the key to my last year of high school. Prioritized right below Mom were the dogs. They'd have to be walked before their owners got home. Felix's owner was no problem; he was nearly housebound with his emphysema and didn't care when Felix got walked, as long as it happened before dark. The others, though—they expected their dogs to be home no later than five o'clock.

May as well have the TV on while I empty the dishwasher and wash the sink full of dirty dishes. A show was on about people who survive on their own in the Arctic wilderness. Amazing, the things they had to do just to get through the day. Did I have it in me to live in such a harsh environment? Could I? Would I?

When the dishes were done, I still didn't know if the woman with the arsenal of weapons would be safe from prowling grizzlies that night. There was a load of clothes in the dryer that really needed to be folded before the wrinkles set in past the point of shaking them out. Mom would be happy if I folded them since she hadn't specifically asked me to. And why not do it in the living room where I could finish watching the show? Turns out it was one of those marathons where they play the whole season in one day. After the first episode, I got lured into the next one. It was hard to tear myself away, but there was justification. I was getting an idea for a possible graphic novel. Someone living in the wilderness. Hallucinations from too much alone time. Maybe even an abominable snowman. Wolves howling at the door. Spending all that time home by myself, I thought I could relate. Before I knew it, another hour was gone, and I was going to have to hurry to give the dogs (or The Boys as I called them) the hour they had coming.

Buster, the one-eyed Chihuahua, was easy to collect. The fence between my backyard and the backyard where he spent most of his life had a loose board. If I lifted it, he'd come charging through, mad for any distraction from endless days of boredom.

Felix was next on my route, and he was an easy handoff. He scrambled on three legs faster than most dogs with four. After that, about a block away and across the street was Jennifer's house. Jennifer, the white poodle, was a *male* dog with an inexplicable name. I took the key from its hiding place and went inside. Sometimes Jennifer was in his dog run, but he could always hear the key turning, and he'd dash through the doggie door, blazing with excitement. He'd walk right up to the hook in the kitchen where his leash hung and wait for me to clip him in. Poor Jennifer. Sometimes I'd call him Jim just to boost his ego a bit.

The first block was usually pretty slow since all three of The Boys stopped every few feet to mark their territory. After that they normally settled down and were ready to actually walk. Only rarely did I have to use one of the plastic baggies I kept in my back pocket.

>>>

I'd been walking for about thirty minutes when a new red SUV drove up, slowing as it passed. Alana was in the passenger seat, and she rolled down the window and waved.

"Hi, Hudson!"

Bryce Something, behind the wheel, waved even

though he probably didn't know who I was.

They turned right on the next street. I knew the area well enough to be aware of a path that connected the two parallel streets. If I cut through it, I could come out the other end just after they drove by. I figured Bryce Something was driving Alana home. Why did I care to see what street she lived on? Just curious, I suppose.

But my timing was off so I came out ahead of them. I was also unaware, until it was too late, that someone's sprinkler runoff had turned the path into a mess of mud, devastating mostly to Jennifer's snow-white paws.

"Hi, again!" Alana yelled out the window. "The dogs are so cute."

They pulled into a driveway about two houses past the shortcut while I fumbled and yanked The Boys back down the same muddy path. To any outside observer, I must have looked like either a stalker or a complete fool. At least Jennifer was enjoying himself. He foraged through the forbidden mud, sniffing the strange substance and ended up with a chocolate brown muzzle to match his feet.

Time was running out to get the dogs back before their owners got home. I jogged along the sidewalk, and The Boys were happy to oblige. Even Felix had no trouble keeping up. After a few minutes the red SUV drove back (without Alana), and Bryce Some-thing waved at me again.

I looked around for something to clean the mud

from Jennifer's paws and snout. I tried rubbing his feet on the grass but that only added a green tinge to his fur. I used the plastic bags, but they were worthless. Finally, I took off my t-shirt and wiped away whatever mud I could.

Back at Jennifer's house I was retrieving the key from the hiding place when the door swung open. Missy, Jennifer's thirteen-year-old owner, looked out in horror at my shirtless self and her muddy, ruined precious pet.

"What happened to her?"

"Um . . . we had a little accident. Sorry, I tried to clean him up."

Jennifer, panting from exertion and excitement, disappeared inside the house.

"My mom's going to be mad," Missy's deadpan voice was chilling. "Jennifer just got groomed last week."

"I'll pay for a grooming," I offered. Jennifer was a great dog, and I would hate to lose their business.

"Do you have any idea how much that costs? More than you make in a week."

To stand there in front of this annoying young girl and have my nose rubbed into the reality of my livelihood was almost more than I could bear.

"*Him.*"

"What?"

"You said *her*, and I'm just saying Jennifer's a *him*."

"Whatever."

She closed the door and left me standing on her

doorstep alone with Buster and Felix. After a few minutes, when nobody came out, I figured I may as well leave. Missy's mom would either fire me, or she wouldn't. My spirits sagged. My brief experience with entrepreneurship was on shaky ground since Jennifer represented thirty-three percent of my dog-walking business. Not to mention the word-of-mouth referrals that probably wouldn't be forthcoming. Fortunately, Felix's owner just laughed at the mud, and I managed to get Buster cleaned up in my bathroom before pushing him through the loose board in the fence.

ALWAYS PLAY HARD TO GET...

. . . when you don't stand a chance with a girl. You still won't get the girl, but at least you won't look desperate. Anyway, that was my philosophy, and I was sticking to it. Alana who? I had a lot of practice playing hard-to-get with girls who weren't interested in me.

The second day of school I arrived before anyone else, including the teacher. Turns out the yoga mat placement assignments *were* permanent. When Alana and Penelope settled on either side of me, they giggled and I wondered whether two days of giggling at the sight of me was enough to solidify it as a daily ritual. To Alana, I was polite, formal, slightly reserved. To Penelope I was attentive, interested, chatty. Although Alana was the acknowledged advanced yoga student, it was to Penelope I turned for questions and encouragement. I'm sure Alana wasn't aware of any of these subtleties.

Penelope was easy enough to be around. I didn't have to strain my brain for witticisms or deep thoughts. Conversation with her was usually one-sided and followed a fairly predictable pattern.

"Oh my God that was the [insert one: 'cutest,' 'most embarrassing,' 'most messed up'] thing ever. Ha ha ha [infuse with soulless monotone]. Literally. You know what I mean? Ha ha ha. Like. Totally. I mean. Can you believe it? [shake head with disbelief] Ha ha ha."

And so on. I admit I was still attracted to her despite the mind-numbing conversation. Who was I to be picky? And she smelled as good as Alana.

After class, it was enough for me to walk with Gus Ligety, and I didn't try to catch up with Alana. When Gus spotted her ahead of us, I warned him off by letting him know she had a boyfriend. Of course, Gus knew who Bryce was. He filled in the last name for me as well as the talk around campus. Bryce was back-up quarterback for the football team the past year and was all but promised the same position for his senior year. Then the coach replaced him with a promising and talented sophomore, bumping Bryce down to third string. Bryce picked up his pride and quit the team which had everyone buzzing. Who would walk away from the varsity football team? Especially during their senior year.

So maybe that was the rebellious side of Bryce

which appealed to Alana. And maybe being rejected in that way allowed Bryce to see beyond Alana's neck tattoo and her messy hair, barriers I initially hoped would make her attractive only to a guy like me.

I COULDN'T STAND WONDERING ANYMORE . . .

. . . so I decided to round up The Boys and go for a walk as soon as I got home from school. Was there going to be a note on Jennifer's front door saying I was fired? If there was, should I bill for the last two walks, or just let it go? By the time we got to his house, I'd already resigned myself to losing Jennifer's business. Felix and Buster panted and strained at their leashes for the friend they could practically smell, he was so close.

There was the note on the door. No surprise. But when I got close enough to read it, the surprise was mine.

Hudson, Missy is home sick from school today. Please ring bell for Jennifer. Carol

Ding dong. Missy opened the door halfway through the *dong* part. There was Jennifer, his pink

36

collar sparkling with rhinestones. His pink tongue lolling with wild anticipation of fun times ahead. Paws and muzzle . . . white as rice. Missy passed me the leash through the door.

"I shampooed him before my mom got home yesterday," she said.

"Thanks." I was truly touched. This girl who seemed to have only hostility for me on the few occasions we met—why would she do such a thing for me?

"Why'd you do it?"

"Who's going to walk Jennifer if Mom fires you?"

I decided not to inform her of the abundance of dog-walkers in our city. Or bother with the fact that either she or her mother were perfectly free to walk him themselves.

"And her name is Jennifer which is why I call her a *her*," Missy continued. Maybe that's why she saved my job. So she could enlighten me on that point. "After Jennifer Aniston."

I wasn't going to touch that one, but before I could think of an appropriate response, Missy let me off the hook.

"I'm supposed to keep the door locked while I'm home alone," she said while closing it firmly on my face. Once again, I was staring at the peephole with my mouth open mid-speech, but this time I didn't wait around to see what would happen next.

Since it was still early, we walked all the way to Alana's house, this time keeping to the sidewalks and avoiding the dirt path. No chance of running into Alana at that hour. I honestly don't think I determined the route of our walk. I think the dogs pulled me along to the spot, two houses down from the location of Jennifer's rapture. The place where Jennifer was finally allowed to become just one of The Boys. Just Jim with muddy paws and nothing else to prove.

ANOTHER WEEK WENT BY . . .

. . . before I heard from Mrs. Dickinson again.

"Hudson?" I immediately recognized her voice, tinkling like a wind chime in the breeze.

Again? This wasn't the way it was supposed to work.

"Mrs. Dickinson, you're calling on my home phone."

"Is that a problem?"

"No, it's just that I was wondering why you didn't call *my* cellphone from *your* cellphone."

"The phone you gave me doesn't work."

"Is it charged?"

"I don't know. I suppose not. I'm not even sure where the darn charger thing is." I could hear the frustration building, so I moved on.

"What can I help you with, Mrs. Dickinson?"

"I need your services for something that qualifies as almost an emergency."

"What's the problem?"

"Lady's gotten out, and I've been calling her, but she's still not back, and it's been over an hour."

Lady was the business I was angling for, so this was perfect timing. After paying Mom the agreed upon rent, there wasn't a whole lot of spending money left over.

"I'll be right there."

"Oh, and Hudson, don't let me forget to give you that phone number. It was in my purse the whole time, wouldn't you know. It's always the last place you think to look."

>>>

I ran into Lady on the way to Mrs. Dickinson's. She was squatting on a neighbor's yard, a few doors away from her home. When I arrived at Mrs. Dickinson's house with Lady cradled in my arms, I was the conquering hero, rewarded like a child with cookies and lemonade.

"Mrs. Dickinson," I said, wiping away some Oreo crumbs with my napkin, "I was thinking maybe Lady needs to get out a little."

"Oh no, that wouldn't be safe. She could get hit by a car," a puff of lavender scent drifted across the table.

"You know I have a dog-walking service."

"Yes, you mentioned that," she said as her eyes narrowed slightly.

"I've been thinking Lady would get along really well with the other dogs, and she might enjoy being out in the fresh air. It'd be good exercise."

"I keep her very healthy. She's not an ounce overweight." The pride in her voice probably extended to her own slim figure, because Lady was definitely on the chunky side.

"No, she's not overweight, I didn't mean that. Her coat is really shiny, and she looks healthy."

Mrs. Dickinson smiled.

"But she could be around other dogs and socialize a bit. And maybe she wouldn't be tempted to run away next time if she got a good workout every day."

"The other dogs. How could I be sure they wouldn't give her fleas or fight with her?"

"They're all great dogs, very friendly. And none of them have fleas or anything like that. I'd never put Lady in a situation where she could be attacked or come home with fleas."

Mrs. Dickinson looked skeptical. She put down the delicate china cup from which she'd been sipping her tea. "Truthfully, I do feel a little guilty leaving her home alone so much when I'm off enjoying myself at the Senior Center," she said. "Maybe we could do a trial period and see how she does."

I came home with a new dog client and the phone number for a possible new client for my other business. I decided I needed names for both businesses that could summarize in a few words what I was never able to do with sentences and paragraphs.

"Canine Cardio" came quickly, but that was the easy one.

"Senior Services." (Too vague, and what if a non-senior wanted to sign up? Doubtful.)

"First Call." (I didn't actually want to be the first call for anything, so scratch that.)

"Hudson's Helping Hand." (A little cheesy but possible . . . kind of vague.)

"Rent-A-Grandson." (Nah, grandsons were expected to do all kinds of crappy chores.)

"Distress Dial!" It wasn't perfect, but it did summarize my service succinctly and alliteratively which was always a plus. "Distress" seemed like a good word, just below the level of an emergency.

Distress Dial and Canine Cardio. Just naming them felt like a big step forward.

>>>

His name and his phone number. That's the only information I had on Mr. Pirkle. Mrs. Dickinson did say he didn't live in our neighborhood, which was something to consider because I didn't have a car on the weekdays until Mom got home from work. But I reasoned that chances were he wouldn't call if he paid attention to the benefits of my service. I'd have to make everything clear so I didn't wind up with another Mrs. Dickinson. And if there ever was a sub-emergency before Mom got home . . . well, I'd have to come up with cab fare out of pocket. I still wasn't sure what to do if someone called between seven and nine in the morning when I was in school. But that seemed unlikely, and besides, Mom was at home until eight, so she could cover for at least one hour. No reason to mention that to her though, since it was probably never going to happen. If worse came to worst, I'd take a cut, and once I turned eighteen, I could legally sign myself out of class.

I dialed Mr. Pirkle's number and waited . . . four, five, six rings . . . I was just about to hang up when he answered.

"Yes?"

It's a positive word, for the most part, but it is still a little distracting when it's the first thing you hear on the other end of a phone call. "Yes" to me, means: *why are you bothering me?*

"Oh, hello, sir. This is Hudson Wheeler of Distress Dial. I received your number from Mrs. Dickinson who mentioned you might be interested in our service." I lowered the timbre of my voice and threw in the plural possessive, hoping it made my business sound more legitimate.

Silence. Then his much deeper voice, which actually sounded pretty youthful.

"Oh, yes. Now I remember. Distress Dial."

"Yes, sir." Some adults get embarrassed when I call them sir or ma'am which is what my parents taught me to say. Not Mr. Pirkle.

"When can you be here?"

Be there? *Already?*

"Do you . . . need me for something right now?"

"Don't we have to formalize the arrangement? Sign a contract? I'd like to get started right away."

Relief and apprehension. Relief. At least he didn't have a problem I had to take care of, and I didn't have to sell him on the business. Apprehension. Contract? Would he be disappointed when he saw that I was just a kid. And why the big hurry?

"Would it be okay sometime after five thirty?"

I'd have the car then and could swing by the store on the way to pick up a prepaid cellphone for him.

"Make it six. I eat dinner at five thirty."

"IF YOU HAD TO DESCRIBE THEM IN ONE WORD..."

I hate it when people say that. As if it were possible to describe a human being in one word. But *if* you were forced to—say somebody challenged you—the word would be "imposing." Mr. Pirkle was imposing in every way. Why did this man want my service? I'd be more likely to call *him* in case of an emergency.

For one thing, there seemed to be about a foot height differential between us, although it was probably less than that. He had a full head of hair with alternating waves of silver and white. His eyebrows and mustache looked interchangeable, like you could just rotate them around on his face and not notice the difference. His eyes alternated between blue and gray as rapidly as a spinning pinwheel. Even his nose was imposing, jutting down from between his eyebrows, pointing towards his mouth as if to say, "be quiet and listen to what comes out of here."

He had that straight-spine bearing I recognized from my dad. The posture of a military man, I was willing to bet on that. I did some quick calculations in my mind and figured him for either a Vietnam vet in his late sixties, a Korean War vet in his late seventies, or a World War II vet in his late eighties. I knew my war history, thanks to Dad. I just didn't know how to guess the age of anyone over fifty.

My question soon had an answer.

"I'm ninety years old, Hudson, and I could use a little peace of mind. Heard you were a good man and always around to help out a guy in a tight spot."

He shook my hand vigorously, nearly crushing my bones. I was completely intimidated, but I rallied quickly, explaining the function of the cell phone, the lifeline that connected him to me. He didn't have any problem grasping my explanation, and he plugged the phone into the wall to begin charging.

It was hard for me to summon the seriousness I felt was required in his presence, but I did my best, reminding myself it was *him* who needed *me*. He was formal but polite and insisted on cutting a check for my first month's pay even though I always billed for the month prior.

When he went upstairs to get his checkbook, I took the opportunity to look around the room. To be honest, it was pretty sterile. The house was small, but newish, unlike Mrs. Dickinson's house, which seemed loaded with history. The furniture looked generic and kind of depressing. You could tell a woman didn't live there. An ashtray on the coffee table showed no sign of ever being used. A picture on the wall looked exactly like one I saw in a hotel once when Mom and I were on vacation. A whole collection of Reader's Digest condensed novels sat on the bookshelf. How was it possible, I wondered, to hide yourself so well in a room where you lived?

I heard his footsteps coming down the stairs, and then I heard the exhalation of his breath, imposing, like everything else about him. Just before he entered the room, a slice of sunlight cut through the shuttered window, catching a glint of glass in the dark corner of a bookshelf. I took a step forward to get a better look and saw the tiny framed picture of a small girl. She grinned from beneath a halo of ringlets. Her clothing, I could tell, was from long ago.

>>>

Mr. Pirkle lived about six miles from my home. Close enough to get to on my bike if necessary, especially if I used the canal trail that connected us more directly than the city streets. But it wasn't a part of our town I normally visited. In fact, I knew nobody on this side of town except Griffin, and whenever we got together he usually came to my house because he missed the old neighborhood.

The house directly across the street from Mr.

Pirkle's had a basketball hoop set up in the driveway.

When I was leaving, the biggest girl I'd ever seen was outside shooting hoops. There were girls on my high school volleyball and basketball teams who were tall, but this girl was an Amazon. Definitely six feet, probably more. And strong. Even the dark brown braid down her back was thick and muscular. There was nothing about her that would be considered feminine, and yet she was. Of course, she was female, therefore "feminine," but she was pretty too. And graceful, the way she moved and jumped to make the basket. Her arms and legs were amazingly toned and copper-colored. She wore really short shorts and a tight tank top. I had to avert my eyes to keep from staring, which was my natural inclination. I could have stared at her all day long.

She bounced the ball a few times before allowing it to leap into her strong and capable hands. Then she raised her eyes to observe me as I tried to slip into the car without being noticed. This girl, whoever she was, had obviously never had the option of not being noticed a day in her life.

She pulled the back of her arm across her forehead to wipe away the sweat that darkened her hairline.

"Hi," she said in the most natural way, as if we were next door neighbors ourselves. Her voice was rich and low, like the oboe I'd unsuccessfully tried to master in middle school.

"Hi," I squeaked back, smacking my head on the door frame while lowering myself into the driver's seat.

IT TOOK A FEW WEEKS . . .

. . . but my muscles did eventually loosen up, and aspirin was no longer a post-yoga habit. I was actually starting to feel some benefits from yoga, which I honestly never expected having thought it was just something girls did to be cool. Gus Ligety and I were the only guys remaining in the class, the other two having apparently realized it wasn't everything they hoped it would be. With the new shrunken class size, Gus had maneuvered several spaces closer to me, like a pawn in a chess game moving in on the queen. Due to his closer proximity, Gus and Penelope got in lots of talking time before and after class. Because he pretended to hang onto her every soulless *ha, ha, ha,* Penelope rewarded him with her nearly undivided attention.

I can't say I minded. I wasn't ready to butt antlers

with Gus over Penelope. I'd reached my tolerance level for her days earlier. Occasionally Alana would unwind herself from an advanced yoga pose like the sleeping yogi (which was an amazing thing to see) and share a secret smirk with me. It's funny how something as simple as a shared secret smirk could brighten my day. But Alana was with Bryce, that much was clear, and maybe because of that, I started to relax. I dumped the hard-to-get playacting like unnecessary baggage. Something happened during all those fifteen-minute passing periods. Alana and I became friends.

>>>

"So then I said to him . . . you call that a joke? You'd better go back to clown school." Gus Ligety smiled fondly at the memory of his clever putdown.

"No!" Penelope gasped. "You did not."

The four of us moved through the hallway as one, Gus, Penelope, Alana, and me.

"I did."

"Oh my God, you're crazy. Ha, ha, ha."

"And you're sweet enough to eat."

"Ha, ha, ha. Oh my God, you're too cute." Penelope slapped Gus on his shoulder, which actually looked painful, but Gus didn't even flinch.

Alana sent out an invitation for a shared secret smirk but I pretended not to see. Try as I might to feel superior to Gus, I suspected one of us would finish up the school year with a girl, and it wasn't going to be me.

Our group split into two when Alana and I arrived at art class. I started walking towards the side of the classroom where I always sat when Alana grabbed my arm.

"Come sit with me," she said, pulling me towards her table.

"What about Bryce?" I didn't see him there, and he was almost always there before us.

"He dropped the class," she said, her mouth turned down in a mock pout.

"Why? What happened?"

"I don't know if you heard about that whole football thing . . ."

"Gus said something about it."

"Yeah, well, Bryce quit the team when the coach gave the backup quarterback position to that sophomore kid, Wyatt. Then in the last game Wyatt got his shoulder separated and . . ."

"Colin, the starting quarterback tore his ACL. I heard."

"So the coach called Bryce and begged him to come back. I told him he shouldn't do it, but he wanted it badly. He said he couldn't play football and carry a full load, so he dropped art."

"But he didn't drop you," I said half-hoping, as though Alana and football couldn't coexist in someone's world.

"He didn't drop me." She jabbed me playfully in the ribs as I sat myself down in the new starting quarterback's chair.

It was great working next to Alana like that, glancing over from time to time to see how her project was coming along. We were working on reflections, and Alana's sketch was a self-portrait of her looking into the humped side of a spoon. Mine was a wild turkey pecking at his own reflection on the side of a car. Once, I looked up and noticed Alana watching me intently.

"That's amazing, Hudson," she said like she really meant it. "You're so talented."

Our teacher walked by at just that moment. "Yes, he is," she agreed.

I was in Heaven.

After class, it was as though our friendship had taken a step to the next level, if there is such a thing as a level between friendship and love.

"You wanna meet me after school?" she asked. "We can hang out. Bryce's busy with football."

I didn't exactly want to be *that guy* who was free after school while the other guys had football practice, but since I was, it was hard to say no. If I focused when I got home, I could get everything done and have a free afternoon.

"Why don't you come to my place?" she suggested. "You know where I live, right?" I blushed at the memory of the first time I walked by her house. "Bring the dogs, and I'll walk back with you. It'll be fun."

I knew what I was to Alana, just a friend. But

having her to myself in art class . . . winning her praise . . . being invited to her place after school . . . priceless. The rational side of my brain told me to put the brakes on, or at least not to totally give in to my fantasies. But the irrational side commanded my heart to deliver hormones at super-optimal levels. I ran around the house like a superhero on steroids, accomplishing everything I needed to and more by the time school let out for Alana.

I even had time left over and enough inspiration to tackle my graphic novel. The last attempt involved an ice monster in the Arctic Circle, but it went nowhere. This time I started playing around with characters like the walking-talking popcorn, sodas, and candy bars you see onscreen before the movie trailers. Only these characters had more depth and complexity. Difficult relationships and existential angst. It could work. At least I was finally doing *something*, and it felt great.

A LATE-NIGHT PHONE CALL IS THE THING PARENTS DREAD THE MOST...

. . . or so my mother tells me. But for me, a late-night phone call is filled with endless possibilities. So when my cell phone buzzed and lit up around midnight, I was psyched. Was Alana calling to talk after the full afternoon we'd spent together? She'd been waiting for me in her front yard when I arrived with the dogs. Never in my life did I have so much to say to another person in such a short period of time. We just clicked, and I think both of us were aware of that by the time her dad picked her up from my place on his way home from work.

So I was thinking Alana, but what I got was Mr. Pirkle. At least, I knew it was him from the Caller ID on my phone. Otherwise, I never would have guessed. The voice was muffled and pretty much incomprehensible. It alternated between too loud and barely audible. There was a roaring, almost electronic background noise you get when somebody's walking around with a phone in their pocket. So he butt-dialed me. I tried yelling and even whistling, but he couldn't hear, so I hung up and went back to sleep.

The next morning, Friday morning, he called me just after the bell rang at the end of art class. Alana was waiting to tell me something.

"Hudson, Pirkle here," he said. "Sorry to bother you, but I wonder if you could stop by. I think there's a problem."

"What's wrong, sir? Do you want me to call for help?"

"No, no, just come by. Nothing I want to discuss over the phone."

I thought about the walk home and the long bike ride over to his house. I couldn't let him know it was a big deal for me. It had to seem effortless. Still I wish he'd give me a clue as to the problem. I hoped he wouldn't turn out to be another Mrs. Dickinson.

"Would it be okay if I was there in an hour?"

"Of course. I'm not going anywhere. Just get here as soon as you can."

Alana tapped her foot impatiently. She had three minutes to get to her next class.

"So do you want to do something tonight?" she asked. "Bryce has a football game, and you know I can't stand football."

"Sure. How about I call you after school?"

"Let me call you," she said. "Bryce and I are going to hang out after school for a while."

>>>

By the time I got to Mr. Pirkle's house, I was drenched in sweat, having beat every speed record I ever dreamed of setting. I rolled the bike into his driveway and leaned it against a hedge.

Inside, Mr. Pirkle was a mess, and I wondered what happened to "imposing." The word of the day would be "flustered" or maybe "agitated." The tidy room I'd observed during my last visit was a disaster. Books on the floor. Ashtray in pieces. Sofa pillows upturned. The picture of the little girl was missing.

"What happened?" I asked the second I walked in.

"I'm not sure," he spoke slowly, as though going over the events in his head. "I think I've been robbed."

"Did you call the police?"

"No, this is none of their business," he snapped.

I took a deep breath while carefully choosing my next words. This wasn't what I'd bargained for when I came up with Distress Dial. The idea of forgotten passwords and runaway dogs seemed very appealing at that moment.

"I don't mean to be disrespectful, but it *is* the business of the police if you've been robbed."

He just gave me *the look*. I'd come to know *the look* very well in the next few months but this first time, well I just crumbled under its weight.

"Do you have a burglar alarm?" I asked, but I already knew the answer. I'd seen the keypad in his kitchen during my first visit.

"Yes . . . I . . . I'm not sure if I turned it on last night before I went to bed."

"Were there any broken windows?"

"Nope."

"How do you think they got in?"

"I've been asking myself the same question all morning. Maybe I forgot to lock the back door last night?"

"Did they take anything valuable?"

"I don't believe so."

"Did your neighbors hear or see anything?"

"I don't know my neighbors well. But I'm sure if they saw something, they'd have let me know."

"And you didn't hear anything either? It didn't wake you up?"

He hesitated for just a moment too long before answering. "No, I didn't hear anything."

This wasn't going anywhere. I couldn't imagine why someone would break into his house in the middle of the night and turn his living room upside down but not steal anything. And then leave the whole rest of the house undisturbed.

"Okay," I finally said. "What do you think we should do?"

"You're the professional," was his unreasonable answer. "What do you think? Clean up, I suppose."

So clean up we did. And we talked. It was the first

glimpse I got into the cracks of Mr. Pirkle's imposing exoskeleton. And it was only later that night I remembered the midnight call.

When I left, the girl was in the driveway again, methodically shooting hoops. The Amazon. Every step she took looked like it had been choreographed. She paused long enough to wave before resuming her shot-in-progress. I wondered what she was doing home from school so early, but she could have been a college student for all I knew. I returned her wave and swung my leg over the seat of my bike.

"What's your name?" she called from across the street.

"Hudson." I balanced on the bike with my feet already on the pedals.

"What's your first name?" she asked.

"Hudson."

"What's your last name?"

"Wheeler." It was beginning to feel a little like an inquisition. I glanced up and saw Mr. Pirkle watching us through the little window above his kitchen sink.

"Why are you always going over to Pirkle's house, Wheeler? You his grandson or something?" She dribbled the ball while speaking.

Wheeler?

"He's my client." I was majorly overpowered in this conversational match. I still didn't even know her name.

"Client? You a lawyer or something?"

I seriously wondered if I looked like a lawyer to

her. In my t-shirt and jeans. Riding my bike. I was turning eighteen in a week, but everyone always said I looked young for my age. But her eyes were sincere and truthful like a little kid's. I could tell she wasn't messing with me.

"No, I'm not a lawyer. I have a business . . . for older people. Distress Dial." Even as I said it, I suspected it would only open up a whole new round of questioning. Maybe I should have said I was his grandson and let it go at that.

"Distress Dial," she took a shot and the ball swished through the net. "You never know," she said. "I saw a show on TV about a kid who graduated from Harvard law school when he was seventeen."

Mr. Pirkle was still staring out the window, so I moved my bike over to her side of the street.

"That's pretty young. I'm seventeen myself."

"Me too," she took another effortless shot. "Half day?"

"Huh?"

"Teacher work day? Is that why you're out?"

"Oh! No, I'm only taking two classes this year. I homeschool."

"Cool," she looked me up and down. "Religious?"

"Nah, I . . ." I stopped myself. This whole thing was too one-sided, and it was time for me to take some control. "Half day for you?"

I thought about Alana, who I'd be seeing in a few hours. The gauzy thing she wore to school which sort of floated over her soft curves. The flowering vine on the side of her neck that seemed to give off a whiff of lavender (or was I just transposing Mrs. Dickinson's scent to Alana's vine?). I thought about the conversation we'd had the day before—sharing our deepest thoughts as if we'd known each other forever. There wasn't a single topic that led to a dead-end with Alana. Certainly none that led to the rocky dirt path I was traveling at that moment.

"Yep." Bounce. "Love it." Bounce.

"And what's your name?"

Go boy, you're on a roll.

"Lauren Fritz, but you can call me Fritzy. Everyone does."

"Okay, well. Nice to meet you, Fritzy. I'd better get going."

"Wait! You never told me what you do for Pirkle."

I looked across the street, thinking it would be an untrustworthy thing to speak about my client to a stranger, even if it was only to confirm his business. But he wasn't looking out the window anymore so I relaxed a bit.

"It's a business I have where I help out mainly elderly people who live on their own. You know . . . anything that falls just below the level of an emergency."

"Are you going to be a doctor?" Bounce.

"No. It's not medical or anything like that. Just . . ." Oh how I hated trying to explain my business to myself and others.

"Oh, like . . . handyman stuff?"

"No, not that either." Maybe it *was* that. Maybe I was just a rent-a-grandson, after all.

"Like when something's wrong but not wrong enough to call 911?"

"Exactly!" It was such a relief to hear someone other than me put it into words. I hiked myself back on the seat of the bike and spun the pedals backwards.

"So what's wrong with Pirkle?" Bounce. Bounce.

"Nothing. I mean, I can't talk about it."

"I get it. Client confidentiality. Saw this show on TV where the lawyer's in bed with a stranger, and he reveals something about his client that leads to a whole thing that eventually gets him killed."

"Yeah, something like that. Only not quite as dramatic." I steered my bike in a tight circle as though it was a racehorse chomping at the bit to get out of the gate. "Guess I'd better go," I said for the second time.

"Wait. How about a game of HORSE before you leave, Wheeler?"

Now, I wasn't a kid who was raised with a manly influence, although my mother did her best. Dad was definitely a man's man, but he was gone so much, and then he left us so soon. All those things a boy learns from his father, well . . . I missed out on most of that. Sure, I knew what HORSE was—a game that had something to do with basketball. Even if I didn't know, I probably could have figured it out after spending five minutes in Fritzy's presence. But did

I know the rules? Did I know the proper form for shooting a ball? Could I even make a basket one out of five times? The answer was no, no, and no.

"I really have to get back," I said. "I have a date tonight," I added for a manly explanation that hopefully would appease her.

"C'mon," she said. "Just one game. Then we'll throw your bike in the back of my truck and I'll give you a ride home."

I knew she wasn't purposely trying to emasculate me. Just one look in those sincere and candid eyes convinced me of that. But at that point her intent didn't matter. I was already there.

"You start," she launched the ball at me, knocking the wind out of me as it made contact with my stomach.

"Oh. Yeah." *Think, Hudson. What do I do now?*

I took a wild guess and tried to throw it in the basket. Naturally, it didn't even come close. To give her credit, Fritzy didn't gloat. In fact, she looked downright disappointed.

"Okay, now me." She'd already retrieved the ball and was holding it in her hands. She took her shot and of course swished it right through the net.

"H," she said glumly.

I'm not an idiot, so I obviously knew she was ahead. I also knew H was the first letter of "horse" and either she just won it, or I did. For some reason, I thought I probably won it for missing. "Horse" didn't seem like a title we'd be fighting over. The ball bounced right back into her capable hands, and she launched it at me again. This time I was prepared and caught it without the aid of my stomach. When she didn't make a move after a few seconds, I started to take another shot.

"You have to take it from where I'm standing," she said.

"I know," I said, but I didn't know. I walked morosely to the spot and took another shot, missing again. She intercepted the runaway ball that was heading for the street. She took her shot and made it. No surprise.

"C'mon, you're not trying," she said irritably.

Which was really humiliating because I *was* trying. Obviously Fritzy couldn't imagine any guy as hopeless as me when it came to sports. Everyone should have her skill.

The cycle repeated, with the only good thing being that I figured out the rules of the game on my own, without having to reveal my ignorance. And by that point it was almost certain I was about to become the Horse.

"R," I beat her to the punch that time. If I was going to be the Horse, then I might as well crown myself with the title.

"Look, Wheeler. Plant your feet so your body doesn't move relative to the hoop. You're swaying all over the place."

She wanted competition, and I wasn't giving it to her. She could have been playing against herself. A slow burn started inside me. This wasn't *my* idea. She forced my hand by offering me the ride home. Who did she think she was, anyway? I didn't care about her stupid game, and now she was getting under my skin and about to ruin my night with Alana. I shot and missed again. She shot and made it again.

"S!" I almost yelled at her. I threw the last ball without even bothering to aim (what was the difference?), and it flew into the street. "I'm outta here," I said. "Now I'm going to be late." Fury colored my cheeks.

"Wait, Wheeler!" she called after me. "I can give you a ride home."

I didn't even turn around to acknowledge her. I was the wimpy kid running home to Mommy.

A SLOW BURN CAN TURN INTO A RAGING WILDFIRE...

. . . if you're not careful. And that's exactly what happened.

Mom was nice enough to go out with her friends that night. She knew I was doing something with a girl, no specific plans. I guess she figured we'd probably end up at my house at some point. Mom isn't a hoverer, and a date for me with a girl was a big enough deal that she wanted to make everything perfect.

But my peace of mind was destroyed by that dumb game of HORSE with Fritzy. It ate away at me all afternoon, and I was only slightly appeased by Alana's call.

"Is your mom home? I'll be over in an hour," she'd said.

Almost exactly an hour later, Alana showed up at my door, a six-pack of assorted microbrewery beers in hand.

"Woah!" Something I wasn't expecting. "How'd you get those?"

"My dad. He belongs to a beer-of-the-month club."

"How'd you get here?" I envisioned Alana walking the streets, hiding the six-pack under her sweater.

"My dad dropped me off."

"He doesn't care if you drink?"

"Why would he? We travel overseas a lot, and in most countries the legal age is eighteen, which I already am. The drinking age here is a joke." She walked past me, tired, I suppose, of standing in the doorway where it must have seemed like I was guarding the gates to the Palace of Innocence. "Want one?"

I accepted one of the chilled bottles, wondering what Mom would think if she came home and found us drinking unsupervised. She was pretty cool, but this could be pushing the limits. I had no way of knowing since it was all new territory for me. Mom and I skipped the drinking-with-girls-in-the-house talk. Alana followed me into the kitchen where we popped open the beers and tilted the first swallows into our expectant mouths.

"Anything interesting on TV?" she asked. "Or we could rent a movie or something."

"How long can you stay?" I wondered whether

Bryce would be expecting her for some post-game victory celebration or a loss consolation (which is what I was really hoping for).

"As long as I want."

"Bryce? Does he know you're here?"

"Of course. He's cool with it. He knows we're just friends. In fact, he's happy I have something to do so I don't nag him about football."

Somehow I didn't want Bryce to be happy that Alana was with me, distracting herself while he attended to the macho business of football. I would have liked him to be concerned, maybe even a little threatened. It would be even better if Alana had lied to him about where she was because she knew he couldn't handle the competition. But no. He was happy.

She sprawled out on the sofa and continued working on her beer. I sat in the arm chair next to her. The cold bottle in my hand felt good on that hot summer night.

"Hudson," she said after a gulp. "Do you ever feel suffocated in this town? I mean, you've spent your whole life here, right?"

The truth was, I *did* feel suffocated. Often. But I also felt a sense of loyalty. Alana traveled around from town to town, country to country. What could she know about belonging to a community with all its faults, but also its rewards? What could she know about making peace with a preschool crybaby like Gus Ligety, growing up with him, accepting the things about him that drove other people crazy because you know how they all began? She couldn't possibly know what loyal friends could be made out of people who ate paste with you in Kindergarten, sniffed scented markers with you in second grade, and dug holes with you in the playground at recess. She couldn't know how a school could rally around a ten-year-old boy to make him feel not so alone when the terrible news came that his father had been killed in action on the battlefield.

"Sometimes," I said. "But it's a good place to grow up."

"Yeah, maybe to grow up." She was flat on her back now, and her braless shape was perfectly visible. A glossy sheen of sweat covered her arms and chest just below her neck. I could see a dewdrop of perspiration in that dip just above her lip. "I don't know. I'm glad that it's senior year and I'll be out of here soon, though. What about you, Hudson? What have you decided about next year?"

I finally felt comfortable enough around Alana to tell her the truth. "I'm not sure, but not college. Not for me."

"I kind of figured that," she said. "Maybe that's what I picked up on about you with the homeschool and all. I feel the same way. Life's too short, and I want to travel and go places. Have . . . *experiences*."

"Yeah, me too. Experiences." I wasn't really sure what that meant since I hadn't thought that far ahead.

She got up and walked to the kitchen and came

back with two new bottles of beer, handing one to me before reclaiming her spot on the sofa.

"Hey, Hudson, wouldn't it be cool if we traveled together? Traveled around the world just working here and there for a few months until we made enough money to go on to the next place? Just, like . . . throwing a dart at a map of the world and going wherever it landed?"

The nearness of her beauty, the sultry night, and the cold beer in my hand . . . It all drew me into her fantasy. Her dream, not mine.

"That would be so cool," I said, honestly believing at that moment it was exactly what I wanted to do. That I had been planning it for, in fact, my entire life.

"A coral atoll surrounding a blue lagoon. Fishing for your dinner and drinking coconut juice. Mangoes for breakfast every single day," I said dreamily. I pictured Alana, bare naked, emerging from the water in slow motion; droplets clinging to her flesh, unwilling to let go until the last minute when cruel gravity forced them to fall away from her soft skin.

She looked over at me as though someone just woke her from a dream. "Yeah, that would be nice for a *little* while," she said half-heartedly. My fantasy, not hers. "But don't you want to visit the major cities? Just feed off of the river of humanity? There's so much to learn from others. So much to see. Wouldn't you be excited to see all the greatest art from every culture around the world?"

I *wanted* to be excited about seeing the greatest

art from every culture around the world. For *her* sake. But the truth was, the only art I cared about at that point was my own. I wanted *my* art to be the greatest art.

And then, as if reading my mind, she asked me, "Can I see your graphic novel?"

I squirmed uncomfortably, but hopefully not visibly.

"It's not very far along yet," I said. "And I have a lot of revisions to make."

"Please, Hudson! Don't worry, I won't judge it as more than a work-in-progress. I'm just curious and really excited for you."

Maybe it was the second beer that allowed me to show it to her. I know I'd have kept it from her otherwise. It was definitely not ready for prime time, but I brought it out from my bedroom and placed it into her hands. She held it so carefully, like it was one of the Dead Sea Scrolls. While I stared at the wall and pretended its surface was of great interest to me, she pored through each of the five pages of my so-called graphic novel. Taking much more time with each page than I knew they deserved.

"I haven't thought out the dialogue yet, so I just put in general ideas and notations," I was already laying the groundwork for a defense. "And obviously, some of the drawings aren't finished, but you get the idea." I knew it wasn't perfect, but the layout was great, and I had ideas for where to go with it.

At the end of what was way too long, she set the

pages down on the table beside her and looked me dead in the eye.

"Hudson. I don't know how to say this exactly but . . . it's beneath you. You're so much better than this."

So maybe she was right. Maybe nobody but me would be interested in that storyline. But I knew the art was good. I knew the panels were laid out effectively and creatively. It felt like a sucker punch to the gut, and I thought about the basketball I'd stopped with my stomach during the game of HORSE with Fritzy. It didn't occur to me hers was only one opinion—at that moment, hers was the only opinion that mattered. I was ashamed.

"Well, thanks, I guess," I mumbled. "It needs a lot of work."

"I don't mean that," she interrupted. "It's just that you're a quality person, and you have so much that's so important to say. Don't sell yourself out by going for something commercial. Speak from your heart."

If I have so much to say that's so important, what is it? What if this is all I have to say? I wondered if Alana was seeing the real Hudson or if she was just seeing a reflection of herself. A guy who would travel the world to bathe in the "river of humanity," or whatever she called it. I was mad at myself for not having something deeper to write about. Something meaningful to other people. Something worthy of her.

"I'm sorry," she said. "Maybe that came out sounding harsh. But I mean it in the most respectful way, Hudson. I have faith in you. One day you're going to write something that'll make people's souls tremble."

Until that happy day, only *my* soul was trembling, and the nagging feeling that all was not right in the world rekindled my slow burn. Alana suggested we get the dogs and go out for a walk, but I thought it unwise to show up at a client's door unannounced with alcohol on my breath. Dogs to Alana were a symbol of stability. She was never able to have one because she never stayed in one place long enough. And as much as she shunned the boring and suffo-cating lifestyle of my town, it seemed to me like she made an awful big deal about dogs.

Because I didn't come up with a better plan fast enough, Alana decided it would be fun if we went to the football game. But instead of sitting in the bleachers and cheering like everyone else in our school, we'd climb up the hill above the stadium and sit under a tree where we could be disinterested observers, poking fun at the whole scene beneath us. Both literally and figuratively beneath us, of course. The loud, brassy squawking of the pep band confined to the far end of the bleachers. The cheerleaders jumping and bouncing around like popcorn kernels in a pan of hot oil. The wave-like roar of the crowd. The occasional angry dad's voice rising above the roar to holler at a son, or a referee. Not for us. We were the future swimmers in the river of humanity. We had important things to do and say. My slow burn got a little warmer.

We sipped at the last bottles of beer which we'd brought with us, warm and flat by that time but deliciously defiant at a high school football game.

"Isn't it wonderful?" Alana said, more than asked. "You can create a beautiful situation out of anything. It's all just how you look at it."

I looked at the flowering vine which ran up her neck and saw the beauty in that, although the artwork was amateurish. Her rumpled hair clung damply to the back of her neck. There was beauty in that too.

"Look, there's Bryce!" She grabbed me by the arm, a little too hard for someone as disinterested in the spectacle below as we were supposed to be. "Look," she pointed to the sideline. "I think he's going to play now, right?"

Although she knew nothing about football, I suppose she knew Bryce well enough to decipher his body posture even from that distance. She could read his pent-up anticipation as he prepared to go in.

"Yeah. Change of possession," I said as indifferently as I could. I downed the last gulp of my beer. "How long do you want to stay?" I asked. "We could go downtown and walk around or something."

"No, let's stay a little bit longer. It'll be funny to see Bryce play."

I didn't know why it would be funny, but she was determined to stay. At least for a while. I still clung naïvely to the belief she saw us as superior somehow to everyone on the field and in the bleachers. That we knew something they didn't. That we shared an important secret.

I stared blankly at the field below. A giant pool of green, lit to daylight proportions by a panel of powerful lights. Like toy soldiers, the players took up their positions. The crowd grew quiet. The snap went to Bryce. He surveyed the field, spotted his opening, and ran for the touchdown. And then all Hell broke loose. The roar of the crowd reached dynamic proportions impossible for me to dismiss without some kind of comment, which I was working on.

"Did you see that?" Alana squealed with delight. "Bryce just scored a touchdown. Right?" In spite of herself and her self-declared antagonism towards the game of football, she broke out in the widest smile I'd personally seen on her pretty face. "Right?" She turned to me for confirmation.

"Yup, he sure did." I didn't want to sound petty and it wasn't the time for sarcasm.

"We're winning, right?"

"Yup," I said again, feeling a little foolish I had nothing better to say. Nothing witty. Nothing insightful. Nothing that could bring us back to the place we'd been just minutes before. Just *yup*.

We're winning, she had said. *Us. Our* school. *Our* team. It wasn't us versus all of them down in the bowl anymore. It was us versus those in the opposing bleachers.

I felt my slow burn rise. The fire spread through my belly. I didn't want to be the outsider looking in. I knew I wasn't going to be the star quarterback in life or anything approaching that. But I wanted to be able to handle myself. Feel comfortable with the physical part of my being. Learn some rules. Be a regular guy. Light up the face of a girl like Alana.

IT ONLY TOOK ME THREE DAYS OF SELF-CRITICISM...

. . . to return to the scene of the crime. *My* crime. I timed it so Fritzy should be home from school, and then some. I had hoped she'd be out in front of her house shooting hoops. I'd be performing a well-check on my client, Mr. Pirkle, and . . . "*Oh, by the way, sorry about the other day. I was rushed with that date thing and all. A little overwhelmed by all the work I had to do. You know how it gets when you're pushing too hard.*"

But when I got there, no Fritzy. Not out front, anyway. I hadn't really intended to check on Pirkle. That wasn't part of our business agreement, and I didn't want him to start thinking it was. I turned my bike towards the direction of home, and got as far as a few blocks away where I'd normally pick up the canal trail. And then I stopped. Another three days of beating myself up? Another three weeks? It was a long ride, and I couldn't exactly afford to swing by here every day on the off chance Fritzy would be outside. And who knows when Pirkle would call me over again? *Pirkle*? I was beginning to sound like Fritzy.

I hesitated. Should I buy some time by knocking on Pirkle's door? Saying I was in the neighborhood? Then maybe when I finished talking to him, she'd be outside. But my bike had a mind of its own and rode into her driveway. Then my legs took over and walked me to her front door.

I could hear the muffled sound of piano music coming from inside the house. Music. A pause. Music. Another pause. Then different music. Real, not amateurish. I wondered if Fritzy was having a lesson. I stood by the door, trying to work up the nerve to ring the bell when it suddenly swung open.

"Hi, Wheeler. What are you doing?" The music continued in the background, louder now that the door was open. I was down one step from Fritzy which made her seem even taller.

"Oh . . ." I was completely unprepared.

"Wondering how I knew you were there? My brother just installed a camera." She pointed up to the tiny white device I hadn't noticed before. "And there's a cool chime that goes off inside our house as soon as someone walks past that bush right there."

I smiled at the traitorous bush as though I was enjoying this new system every bit as much as she was.

"Wow, very cool," my bobble-head bounced with ridiculous approval.

"So why are you here?" she asked again, now that the means of my detection had been explained.

I dumped the straightforward explanation I'd planned. It would have worked in the original scenario where I came across her unexpectedly in the course of my business. But now that I had been foolishly discovered loitering at her front door, I grasped at the first thing that came to mind.

"I was just wondering if you might have seen something last week. Anything unusual around Pirkle—uh, Mr. Pirkle's house. Any strangers hanging around or anything like that?"

"Why? What happened?" her eyes lit up with interest.

"It's nothing. Just wondering. That's . . . all."

"Is he okay?"

"Yeah, yeah. He's fine." I hadn't actually seen or talked to him, but I assumed he was fine.

"Nah. Haven't seen anything."

"Okay, well, thanks then."

"I'll let you know if I do see something."

"That'd be great. Great, then."

"Do you have a business card so I know how to get in touch with you?"

"Oh! Oh, sure." I actually did have a business card, and I fumbled through my wallet to find it. Fritzy took it from me and stared at it for a moment. The music had switched again from amateur to professional. "Someone plays piano." Nothing like stating the obvious.

"My brother. Come on in." She opened the door wider, and I followed her inside.

We walked through the living room where a giant blond child, who was presumably Fritzy's brother, shared the piano bench with a slight, dark-haired man, presumably the piano teacher. I felt a little like Jack (of the beanstalk fame) when he finds himself trapped in the giant's castle. We exited into the kitchen where Fritzy motioned me to a round glass table surrounded by four chairs.

"Want something to drink?" she asked.

"Whatever you're having," I said casually, thinking all the while how to pivot to an apology, or some semblance of one.

She poured two giant glasses filled with eggnog, which I didn't even know could be consumed any sooner than Thanksgiving. I hated the idea of eggnog but tried a sip while Fritzy guzzled down the entire contents of her glass.

"The other day," I said once she set down the empty glass with a satisfied *Aaah*. She stretched out her long legs and leaned back in the chair.

"When you lost the game of HORSE and ran away all mad like a wuss?"

"Yeah, that day." Did this girl not understand the subtleties of doublespeak?

"Yeah, I remember. What about it?" she asked

without the slightest change in the expression of those sincere and candid eyes.

"Well, I'm just sorry about it, that's all. It's been bothering me."

"It's been bothering you this whole time?" she seemed amazed. "You were embarrassed . . . no big deal. I've been there before."

"Thanks," I said. "Thanks for saying that. Even though I don't believe you."

"Hey, I have. So has everyone. What else is new?"

"Anyway, that's the real reason I came over, if you really want to know. To apologize."

"I knew that." She smiled, which I hadn't ever seen her do before. Her teeth were perfect, white and even just like you'd expect them to be. "You wanna play HORSE?" she grinned.

"Sure, I have time for a game, I guess."

"And nothing's wrong with Pirkle?"

"Not that I know of."

"Good deal." She stood up and clapped me on the shoulder. I noticed a tiny dried fleck of egg nog in the corner of her shining, pink, pillowy lips.

"You don't want the rest of that?" She eyed my still full glass.

"Not really. Don't care much for eggnog."

She picked up my glass and took a few swallows before putting the half-filled glass in the refrigerator.

"Can't let it go to waste," she said.

>>>

"Teach me, I'm all yours," I said once we were standing under the hoop.

"Why, Wheeler? Why now?"

"Because I'm sick of being so . . . inadequate when it comes to sports."

"I'll teach you," she said slowly. Thoughtfully. "But you're not going to run off again if I get a little rough, are you?"

I couldn't tell if she was kidding or not because she always looked so freaking sincere.

"I'm not running off anywhere. Let's play."

"All right, then. I guess learning how to shoot is a good place to start. You remember what I told you about keeping your body steady relative to the hoop, right?"

How could I forget? That unsolicited piece of advice was the straw that broke the camel's back. This time I welcomed it and tried to visualize what it really meant.

"Okay, before you take your shot, plant your feet and keep your knees bent. I know this goes without saying, but I'll say it like we're starting from scratch. Hold the ball with your dominant hand, and support the ball with your other hand. When you get the ball up to face-level, release it from your shooting hand by kind of flicking your wrist forward. Imagine reaching into a cookie jar above your head. That's the motion your wrist should be making. Your hand's going to push up and through the ball. Let your fingers put some back-spin onto it. Is that clear?"

She sounded like a gym teacher—a good one. A gym teacher I actually wanted to listen to, not one I did everything in my power to ignore, to put up with until the bell rang. I felt ashamed that when I was young I had tuned out my dad during the precious times he'd tried to share his love of sports with me. But that was then, and this was now. I rehearsed everything she said in my mind, visualizing her words and putting them into action. When I released the ball, just like a homing pigeon, it flew to its nest, arching to just above the rim of the net before dropping down for a perfect swish. Beginner's luck? I didn't care. I was walking on air.

"Way to go, Wheeler." She high-fived me. "Now do it again."

I did it over and over. Making it sometimes. Missing it others. Fritzy never went crazy either way. She was solid and patient through the good and the bad. When we'd both had enough, she went over to the garden hose and turned it on. She drank thirstily and then passed it to me. It tasted deliciously like hot plastic and dirt. I drank like a camel then sprayed the sweat from my face. We sat on the lawn under the shade of her maple tree.

"You know, Wheeler, you're not bad. You're coordinated, I can see by the way you get on and off your bike. You've got reasonably decent muscle tone which can be improved with a little effort. You don't have to be tall to be athletic. There was a guy named Muggsy Bogues who played for the NBA. He was only five-foot-three."

"I'm five-foot-six," I lied.

"Well, yeah, and you're not going to play for the NBA either. I was just saying."

"Thanks, Fritzy." I stood up. "Next time I come by to see Pirkle, I'll look to see if you're home. Maybe you can show me some more stuff, if you're not busy."

"Stop by any time. Doesn't matter if you're coming to see Pirkle. Just knock on my door, I won't bite."

And she didn't.

HAPPY BIRTHDAY . . .

. . . to me. Eighteen. Mom insisted on a party to which she invited my aunt, uncle, two young bratty cousins; Cameron and his ever-present girlfriend Eunice; and Griffin whom I hadn't seen in a month. I surprised myself by inviting Gus Ligety and Penelope, who turned out to be two of my new best friends, at least in school. And Fritzy. I invited Alana first, but she and Bryce were going to a concert with long-ago purchased tickets.

I wouldn't have invited both Alana and Fritzy to my party. I don't know why exactly. Neither was my girlfriend, and neither would be jealous of the other. I guess it was the off chance one of them might say the wrong thing to me about the other. It felt safer to keep them apart.

Fritzy also had other plans, but she canceled

them. In fairness, they didn't involve long-ago purchased-tickets.

"Couldn't pass up your birthday party," she said. "Other people can wait."

"Other people," it turned out, was one of the two giant guys she was currently dating. She didn't talk much about them like other girls did. Any information I had about her dating life, I had to drag out of her. I hadn't actually seen them, but I imagined them as giants. Maybe they were. Maybe they weren't.

The party was what you'd imagine. An outdoor barbecue taking advantage of the still warm summer nights. A cake Mom labored over and served with ice cream. Fritzy showed up in her black Tacoma truck. The one that could have transported my bike home after that first fateful game of HORSE. Griffin, who had transferred to Fritzy's school, was in awe. Fritzy was the star athlete at their school, he told me when we were alone in the kitchen. She had a lock on a full-ride scholarship, the colleges were already circling like vultures. The child's voice that lived inside my head spoke to Alana when I heard that. *I'll match my Fritzy against your Bryce any day,* it said. Everyone at the party was in awe of Fritzy, and she didn't even have to open her mouth to make it happen. Although she did. Plenty. Mainly for eating, but talking also.

For me, the highlight was the present from Mom. Her old car. She bought a new (used) one for herself. At last, I was officially mobile at the age of eighteen. I got other presents too—a basketball from Fritzy; my own yoga mat from Penelope and Gus so I wouldn't have to sit on someone else's "sweaty buttprint," Penelope had explained (ha, ha, ha); a hundred bucks from my aunt and uncle; and some new graphic novels of the variety Cameron, Griffin, and I once enjoyed together. After a year or two they'd lost interest, but I was forever hooked on that medium which told a story with emotional punch and raw intensity like no other.

Everyone stayed really late, chilling on the patio until after midnight. At some point my phone vibrated, and Pirkle's number came up. I went inside to take the call, wondering why he was calling at such a late hour.

"Mr. Pirkle?"

Silence on the other end and then, "Who's this?"

"It's me, Mr. Pirkle. Hudson Wheeler. Is everything okay?"

Another long silence. "Who are you? Why are you calling?"

"You called *me*, Mr. Pirkle. Did you mean to call me?"

"I can see her from here," he said. "Come over to see for yourself."

"See who, Mr. Pirkle?"

Fritzy wandered into the house and stared at me.

"Do you really have to ask? Don't you know what's going on?" Pirkle said.

Then the same noises that come along with a butt dial. Clunking and whooshing. A voice (voices?)

in the background. I hung up and dialed his home phone. It rang and rang. No answer.

"Pirkle?" Fritzy asked. "Something wrong?"

"I'm not sure," I said. "I think he might be drunk and maybe butt-dialed me. He's done it before."

"I was just leaving. When I get home I'll look and see if there's anything unusual. I'll let you know."

The text that came about fifteen minutes later was mostly reassuring.

"Don't see anything strange," Fritzy texted. "Saw a flashlight beam bopping around upstairs for a minute, but now everything's dark."

THE PARTY CONTINUED ON...

. . . into the following week. "You have to let me make it up to you," Alana said. "Your eighteenth birthday! I was so bummed to miss it."

We made plans to meet after school. I'd pick her up in my new (old) car. My time management was way better by then, so the dogs were walked, dishes done, homework almost finished (nothing that couldn't be put off until later), and laundry folded (my careless decision to fold in front of TV that one day went over so well with Mom, she added it to my permanent list of chores).

Then I took another shot at the graphic novel. It was like a dark cloud always hovering over me, raining down dismal thoughts whenever I thought about it. Alana's so-called belief in my superior talent only served to make me doubt every creative thought that popped into my head.

Say something important, the dark cloud dared me. And then it laughed because it knew I had nothing important to say. A walking, talking tub of popcorn threatened by the Diet Coke's attentions to the far more interesting box of Milk Duds? Please. What was next? A jumbo slushy to teach the popcorn how to be a man? The drawings were good, and I stared at them for a long time wondering how a substitute storyline might at least save these characters. But the longer I looked at them, the more I detested them. One by one, I dropped the five pages into the paper shredder. Better that no one else sees this mess. Maybe I'd resurrect the idea of the abominable snowman, howling wolves, and a crazed individual living on the frozen edge of civilization. There must be something important to say in all of that.

Then it was time to pick up Alana, and I found myself in a huge line of cars waiting with all the parents of kids too young to drive. Never having been in that position before, I underestimated the slow progress of the line. By the time I got to the front of the school, Alana was sitting on the grass, slouched against a tree looking hot and neglected. She smiled when I pulled up and leaned over to open the passenger door.

"Hop in!" My cheery disposition was down a few notches by then. I had new compassion for parents who did this every day.

"Hudson! Cool car." Alana buckled her seatbelt,

and we took off. The air conditioner didn't work, so all four windows were down to combat the heat of the afternoon. I turned to look at her, head thrown back, eyes closed, wind whipping her hair into an even greater tangle than usual. I could get used to this picture.

And when I looked back at the road, Alana blindsided me by leaning over and kissing me on the cheek.

"Happy birthday, Hudson," she said, and I melted from something other than the heat in the car.

"How was the rest of your day?" I asked casually, as though it was perfectly normal for me to pick up Alana after school and have her lean over and kiss me on the cheek.

"Okay," she answered unconvincingly. "Kind of sucky, actually."

"Sucky" was not what I wanted to hear on the day I was celebrating my birthday with Alana Love.

"What's wrong?"

"I don't want to talk about it."

I didn't have a lot of experience with girls, but it seemed to me that "I don't want to talk about it" was an entirely unfair tactic used by the female sex. I'd even heard my mother say it on rare occasion. To me, it always felt personal and exclusionary. It also felt like the person who said it really *did* want to talk about it, but they wanted you to drag it out of them. When you ask a guy what's wrong, he'll usually answer and then move on, but at least you're not left guessing. I decided not to let it ruin my day.

"So, you said you had plans for us. Tell me where to go."

"First stop, the mini-mart," she brightened. "Turn in here."

She led me through the front door which had height measurement markers in case the clerk needed to identify a fleeing robber.

"Selfie!" She had us pause at the door marker where I straightened my spine and lifted up a little on my toes to take me to all of five-foot-six. We smiled into her phone camera and she clicked it for posterity. Eighteen.

"Okay, follow me." She walked to the counter and asked for a pack of cigarettes. "It's for him," she said to the clerk, pointing to me. Then she randomly grabbed three or four adult magazines and shoved them into my hands.

"I don't want these," I protested.

"Of course you do. Today only." She turned to the clerk. "How much?"

"I'll need to see some ID," the clerk said.

"Of course you need to see ID!" Alana turned to me, grinning. "Hudson, show the nice man your ID."

I did it gladly because she was getting such a kick out of it. And I must admit when I gave my ID to the clerk and he looked at it and then looked at me, it was kind of a rush. I know I seemed much younger than eighteen, but here I was with a real ID doing something perfectly legal.

Alana laughed and threw her arm around me as we walked out the door. I tossed the cigarettes in the nearest garbage can but kept the porn.

Then it was on to early bird dinner at a local vegetarian restaurant. Would I expect anything else from Alana Love? But, hey, she was paying. By then her mood had slumped again, and she was unusually quiet over dinner.

"So, are you going to tell me what's wrong, or are you going to make me drag it out of you? And by the way, I really don't want to do that."

I tried to laugh it off like I was joking even though I wasn't, but she didn't laugh back. I was a little peeved. This was supposed to be my birthday celebration. She slurped the last of her green smoothie through a straw and then looked up at me with those enormous kitten eyes. Or were they puppy eyes?

"It's nothing, I don't want to be a downer on your birthday." She sighed. "It's just Bryce."

Bryce wasn't invited to my birthday dinner and neither was any talk of him, so I didn't say anything.

"But since you asked," she went on after a pause that didn't lead to any follow-up on my part, "I'll tell you, if you really want to know."

"Sure. Why not?" Could she have missed the disinterest in my voice? Apparently.

"We usually have lunch together, by that tree near the auto shop. You know where it is?"

Of course I knew where it was. I knew exactly

where Alana ate lunch last year when she first came to our school. I wondered whether the more self-conscious you were, the more you were conscious of others. I wondered if Alana knew where Cameron, Eunice, and I ate lunch last year, or where my locker was. I didn't wonder, I knew. She didn't.

"Yeah, I know where it is."

"But ever since football, the guys on the team have been pressuring him to eat with them at their table. You know where that is? Where the two benches are pushed together next to the fountain?"

What did she take me for, a blind man? I was a senior, but unlike her, I'd been cognizant of the social chess game for more than three years.

"Yes, I know where they eat," I answered tersely. The broccoli quiche wasn't quite cutting it at that moment.

"A couple of times I've just gone with Gus and Penelope for lunch and told Bryce to hang out with his football friends. I mean, I don't want to be a drag on him, and I know it'll be over as soon as football season's over."

"Yeah." Somehow, I doubted it would be over then, but I didn't say so.

"I think I've been bending over backwards to give him his space. I'm not exactly the clingy type."

"The clingy type. What does that even mean? I mean if you like someone and all . . ." No I didn't have insight into these types of games, but I threw it out there to see if it would stick. She basically ignored my question and went on.

"And then today he drops it on me that a bunch of them are going away for a week during Christmas break to Hawaii. Some guy on the team, his dad is really rich, and he rented a huge house a block away from the beach."

"Maybe they want to finish up the season with some of that male bonding shit. Could be worse." I envisioned a week over winter break with just me and Alana and nothing to do all day. And no Bryce in the picture.

"That would be fine if it was just male bonding, but there are some girls invited too. There'll be ten kids in all. Six guys and four girls."

"Oh, well . . . not you?" Even better. Maybe Alana would break up with Bryce over this. I just had to be cool and supportive.

"No, not me. Exactly my point."

"So where does that leave you?"

"That leaves me nowhere, which is why we had a big fight today."

I started working on my green smoothie which was suddenly surprisingly tasty.

"What would you do if you were me, Hudson? Do you think I should break up with him if he goes?"

Now, even I knew this was a trap. If I said "yes," then she might question my motives. If I said "no," she stays with Bryce.

"I can't make that decision for you," I shifted the tone of my voice to mature concern. "You have to decide what you can and can't put up with."

Break up with him, I said in my head.

Alana stared down at her soup as though the answer were to be found somewhere in the bowl. Finally she looked up. "He's not like those other guys, Hudson. If he was, you know I wouldn't be with him. He's different. He's like us."

Like us.

"Does he want to travel after he graduates?"

"No. Not like us that way. He's going to college, but I think it's just to make his parents happy."

Not like us.

"Anyway, this is my problem, not yours. It's your birthday. Tell me about your novel. What've you decided?"

"I destroyed it," I said flatly. "You were right. It was crap."

"No! No! You shouldn't ever do that. Keep everything for when you're famous. Someday all your early stuff will be valuable."

I couldn't imagine popcorn-man ever being valuable and my face must have betrayed that.

"Okay, well, what's done is done. But I'll bet you're working on something new. What is it?"

"I have some ideas." I picked up a whole-wheat roll and started gnawing on it. "I'll let you know when it's far enough along."

"Fair enough." Alana pulled her backpack onto her lap and started riffling through its contents. "I have your present. Promise you won't laugh." She pulled out a scroll tied up with a ribbon and passed it across the table to me.

I unwound it carefully. It was a sketch she'd done of me from the neck up, pretty decent likeness. And all around me, the great landmarks of the world— the Eiffel Tower, Pyramids, Leaning Tower of Pisa, Big Ben. As tribute to my fantasy, there was even a tropical island in the upper left corner. A blue lagoon dimpled its center like a thumbprint cookie. The message was clear. This was my future. *Our* future. I'd be her companion, standing in for Bryce who had chosen college over traveling with Alana. I can't say I minded. In fact, I was touched and honored.

DON'T PUT OFF DOING YOUR HOMEWORK...

. . . until late at night, especially if it requires even the smallest amount of creativity, like an art project. But after dinner Alana and I went to a movie, and by the time I got home after dropping her off, even Mom was asleep. For me, going right up against a deadline was typical, so when the phone rang at midnight, I was still wide awake and not even close to being finished. Once again, I thought (hoped) it was Alana, and once again it turned out to be Pirkle. Another butt-dial? Or worse yet, a drunk dial?

"Is everything okay, sir?"

"Hudson, is that you?"

"Yes. Is there something I can help you with?"

"I . . . I'm not sure. I'm not feeling well . . . and I thought if maybe it isn't too much trouble for you to stop by . . ."

"Do you want me to call an ambulance?"

"No, Heavens no. Please. If you could just stop by for a minute, I'll be fine."

I thought about my art project. I thought about the late hour. I thought about the so-called "robbery" and the strange late night calls. I thought about the predictable and easy money that came from walking dogs, and how dogs didn't call you to come over in the middle of the night. I thought about the much more significant stream of income I got from Distress Dial. But I hadn't anticipated people actually using it.

"Of course," I said. "I should be able to make it in ten minutes at this time of night." I hoped the reminder of the late hour might change his mind. But it didn't.

"Thanks, Hudson, sure appreciate it. I'll keep an eye out for you." His voice sounded thin and shaky. Not very imposing.

>>>

When I arrived at Pirkle's house, it was lit up like a Christmas tree. The front door swung open before I could even get out of the car.

"Really sorry to do this to you, Hudson," Pirkle said once I was inside. The picture of the little girl was back on the bookshelf. "I know it's late. And a weekday, at that." He sipped from a glass of what I hoped was water.

"No problem," I waited for an explanation but when none came, I dug. "Were you feeling sick or something?"

Normally, he had a way of ducking his head and squinting when he spoke. Like he was bypassing your skull and looking right at the important stuff inside. But that night his eyes were unfocused instead of the laser beams I was used to. There was something there. Fear maybe.

"I might have been a little sick, I'm not sure." He paused for a minute. "For a second, I wasn't sure where I was. Thought I was back in the old house."

Not knowing how to respond, I said nothing.

"I'm ninety years old, Hudson. Can you believe it?"

It wasn't really a question. I knew he was talking to himself and that *he* was the one who really couldn't believe it. I almost-kind-of knew how he felt because I couldn't believe I'd just turned eighteen. Both of us surprised by our age. As if age is a destination we arrived at without remembering how we got there.

"No, I can't believe it," I said without meaning it. "You look too young to be ninety."

"Ninety," his eyes glazed over. "Can I get you something to drink?"

"No, I'm fine, thanks."

My art project called to me. I'd left a note on my bed in case Mom woke up. I was wound up and slightly resentful. I felt two knots of pain brewing behind my eyeballs. A long, sleepless night loomed ahead of me, and I'd have to stop at the mini-mart for coffee on the way home. I'm ashamed to say of all the things going through my mind just then, Mr. Pirkle was at the bottom of the list.

"What house?" I asked. "What house did you think you were in?"

"Oh." He seemed surprised by the question. "The house I lived in when I was a young man. When I was married."

"You were married? What happened to your wife?"

So maybe not the best way of asking, but I was just plain tired and a little curious.

"My wife? We divorced a long time ago. So long ago that it's sometimes hard for me to remember what she looked like. Funny, huh?"

"Yeah," I said, although I didn't think it was funny. To forget a person who once meant everything to you. Someone you'd once loved enough to marry. I didn't think that could ever happen to me, or at least I hoped it couldn't. I looked at the picture of the little girl.

"So . . . are you okay now?" I leaned forward in my chair to get the ache out of my lower back. "I could call someone to come over, if you want. Is there anyone?"

"If there was anyone to call I wouldn't have called you. That's the point, isn't it? The point of your service?"

I felt like an idiot. Of course it was the point.

"What can I do for you, Mr. Pirkle?"

"Do you know a good story?" he chuckled, but I

knew he was serious.

"A good story? For real?"

"For real? Is that what young people say? Okay, then. Do you know a good story for real?"

He picked up the glass and sipped from it again. His hand trembled, his white knuckles betrayed how tightly he was holding on. He passed his upper lip over the lower one to remove the leftover moisture.

"Okay, a good story," I said, leaning back in the chair. "Let me think for a minute. Could it be a made-up story or should it be real?" I was buying time. I had no idea.

"Since you said *for real*, make it a real story."

He just wanted to hear me talk, so I probably could have said anything. Even made up something, without him knowing it. But I reached back for the story that had always brought me comfort because it was comfort I knew he was after.

"When I was seven years old," I began, "my father was going away. He was always coming and going, so I was used to it. And I knew it would be a long time before I saw him again, but I was used to that too. That was our life. Since he was leaving the next day, he had to run to the store to pick up a few things. I wanted to go with him, but Mom told me I needed to take my bath and get ready for bed. I could wait up for him, she said. And he wouldn't be long. Dad told me he'd bring home a present if I was good and did what Mom said.

"*What do you want?* he asked. And I asked what

I could have. *Anything,* he said. And since he said I could have anything, I went all out and asked for a car. He laughed and said he'd bring me a car.

"I could hardly believe my good luck, so I hurried to get ready. I brushed my teeth, took my bath, got into my PJ's. And then I got in bed to wait for Dad to come back from the store. Mom read me a story while we waited."

Mr. Pirkle was visibly relaxing. He set the glass of water on the coffee table, his hand steady again. He didn't look right at me while I spoke, but occasionally he'd lift his eyes and nod his head to let me know he'd heard what I was saying and wanted to hear more.

"So finally, Dad was home, and he came into my bedroom where I'd been waiting, crazy excited. I thought he'd say something like, *Come out to the garage, son. Your new car is waiting.* That's what I was expecting, as ridiculous as it sounds. But instead, he fished around in the pocket of his jacket and pulled out one of those matchbox cars. You know the kind?"

Mr. Pirkle nodded.

"It was just this little orange sedan-type car with a white stripe that ran the length of the hood and roof. My heart sank, and my face must have too. I actually thought Dad was going to give me a real car. Mom got up and left us alone, and Dad sat down on the side of my bed. He started racing the car up and down the covers of my bed, making these racing engine noises. Then he asked me if I wanted to race it, but I said I didn't. I was still pretty disappointed.

"He put the car on the bedside table and lay down beside me. *Let's take a drive in your car,* he said. *Where do you want to go?* It seemed like a silly idea to me, but I played along with him.

To Disneyland, I guess.

Who's going to drive? he asked. *Me or you?*

Me.

Okay, put on your seatbelt. I'll sit in the back, and we'll let Mom sit up front with you, okay?

Okay. But she has to put on her seatbelt too.

Of course!

"And it went on like that while I pulled out of the driveway and hit the freeway, and somehow the car turned into a convertible and the top was down and the wind was blowing through Mom's hair. It was dark, but the full moon was so bright we could see everything. Then we got to Disneyland and pulled right up to the front where there was a special parking spot that said *Reserved for Hudson Wheeler's special car.* After that, Mickey and Goofy came out the front gate to personally welcome us, and they shut down the whole park so just me and Mom and Dad could go on any ride we wanted with no lines, and all the food was free, and at the end of the evening they had a special parade and fireworks display just for us.

"By the time Dad and I finished the story, which ended with us all coming home and being so exhausted we fell into bed and went to sleep right away, I was pretty happy. A real car didn't seem so important anymore.

"Dad picked up the little car on my bedside table and put it on my pillow. *This car . . . It's a way for you to imagine all the places you want to go and all things you want to do,* he said. *Right there.* He tapped my forehead with his finger. Then he pulled out a picture of me that he kept in his wallet. *It's the same thing I do when I want to be with you. I just look at your picture, and I'm with you no matter where I am or what I'm doing. Right here.* He tapped on the spot right over his heart. And at that moment I had everything I ever wanted."

Mr. Pirkle nodded his head, although he wasn't looking at me. Almost like he knew what was coming next and, who knows, maybe he did.

"When my father died, they told me he was holding onto a picture of me," I said. "So I've always known I was with him when he needed me most."

I'd thought of this story so many times, but I never told it to anyone, not even Mom.

"Your father," Mr. Pirkle said. "Military?"

"Army. He was killed in Iraq."

"It's a shame, Hudson. Your father should have lived to see the fine young man you've become."

"Can I do something else for you, Mr. Pirkle?" I felt completely drained.

"I'm fine, Hudson. You can take off now. Sorry to keep you up so late."

Outside, I sat in my car for a while. I knew what was still waiting for me at home, but I wanted to make sure Pirkle was okay. I thought I'd wait for his lights to go off, but they never did. After about fifteen minutes, I pulled away from the curb and drove home. It had been a long time since I'd felt Dad's presence as intensely as I did that night.

AFTER HALLOWEEN AND BEFORE THANKSGIVING...

. . . I finally figured out the rhythm of homeschooling, and it was perfect for me. I had weekly meetings with the homeschool teacher who worked out of our school district's office. Mrs. Pereira took a relaxed approach and let me take part in creating my own curriculum, especially in English where we had more flexibility. There was assigned reading, but it was tailored towards my interests, and she agreed to let me create a graphic novel for my senior project.

Since I was eighteen, Mom's signature wasn't required on my progress reports, but I always brought them home to show her. They were good, and I hoped they solidified her faith in me. Alana and I hung out two or three times a week after school and always on Fridays when Bryce was busy with football. We never went to the hill above the stadium to watch another game—the weather had turned cold and wasn't ideal. Of course, Alana wouldn't be caught dead in the stadium itself. That just wasn't *us*.

Fritzy and I kept at the mission of turning me into a physical specimen, or at least an approximation of one. We ran, lifted weights in her garage, and played basketball using the middle school court a few blocks from her house. I was a regular at her house. Even the giant, blond, piano-playing younger brother treated me like part of the family in that he ignored me whenever I was around. I wasn't in love with his music, but I did succeed in learning the difference between Bach and Beethoven. Once, in a half-hearted attempt to bond with Frankie, I told him I'd like to take lessons myself. Mr. Scolari, the piano teacher, frequently banished Fritzy and me from the living room, so we continued to drink eggnog in the kitchen. Well, Fritzy did, and I watched.

Jennifer, the poodle, came to stay for a week. Missy's mom was traveling on business, so Missy was sent to stay with a friend during that time. Jennifer, naturally, wouldn't hear of staying anywhere but my house, or so Missy claimed. I charged a sizeable amount for this round-the-clock service, and in return, I looked forward to the pleasure of Jennifer's full-time company. Missy and her mom arrived at my door one day with all of Jennifer's accessories—pillow, sweaters, rhinestone-studded leash, food and water dishes, special diet, etc. Jennifer stood beside them, mysteriously transformed overnight to a shocking shade of pink.

"It's for her birthday," Missy blurted out, reading the horror in my eyes.

"It's temporary," her mom winked at me. "It'll wash out in the next grooming."

"Happy birthday, Jennifer," was the only response that seemed appropriate. In the back of my mind was all the teasing I'd be subjected to over the next week because of my association with the now hot pink Jennifer.

"I don't want that dog just hanging around the house," Mom warned. She wasn't real big on pets, which explains why I never had one of my own. I promised to take Jennifer with me whenever I went out.

>>>

One day after school, I got a call from Fritzy.

"Wheeler, you coming by today? I got two surprises for you."

She refused to reveal them over the phone, so naturally I had to go even though I hadn't planned on it. Her eyes opened wide when she caught her first glimpse of pink Jennifer.

"What the hell is that?"

"*That*," I mustered all the dignity I could, "is my full-time responsibility for the next week."

"What's her name?" she asked, apparently without glancing between Jennifer's hind legs.

"*His* name," I said. "Is Jennifer."

"What the hell kind of a mean trick is that to play on a dog?" she asked.

"Her owner is a young girl," I said by way of explanation.

"You just called him a *her*," Fritzy said accusingly. "And what difference does it make if the owner's a girl?"

"She likes Jennifer Aniston, what can I say?"

"And that's supposed to make it okay?"

"It's *temporary!*" Frustration raised the volume of my voice and the giant child opened the door to determine the source of the uproar in his front yard.

"Can we move on?" I begged. "Tell me what the surprises are."

Fritzy turned her back to me. "Now I don't feel like telling you," she sulked.

"Why is this my fault? I didn't dye him pink."

She turned around and I could see she *had* already moved on. "Well you could've at least stuck up for him," she smirked.

"I do every day," I said. "I call him Jim whenever we're alone."

Fritzy laughed, and it reminded me how much I loved to see her cut loose. Yup, we were that close, arguing the way I imagined brothers and sisters would. The giant child retreated into his house, closing the door behind him.

"So the first surprise is that I signed us up for a coed basketball league." She started to throw the ball to me but then stopped. I'm guessing it was the sight of the rhinestone-studded leash looped around my wrist.

"You think I'm ready for that?"

"Of course you're ready. It's a coed league so we'll be playing together. I'll have your back."

A real team playing a real sport. I hadn't done that since fifth grade. Who would've thought I'd be on my way so soon?

"Okay, if you say so. What's the second surprise?"

"I got you a new client."

"Dog walking?"

"No. A new *real* client. For Distress Dial."

Fortunately, Jennifer didn't know enough to take offense.

"A lady I met when I was volunteering for the library's used bookstore. We got to talking, and she told me how she lives by herself, and I suggested your service."

That was big. A substantial new income stream.

"Did you get her number?"

"Of course. What do you take me for?"

"So . . . can you give it to me?"

"Sure but . . ." she swished the ball into the hoop. "I think we should call on her in person, and I'd better go with you. She told me to come by, and since she already knows me, I could introduce you. It'd be better that way, you know." Throw. Swish. "Set her at ease. Then you move in for the close."

"All right. Can we go now?"

"I really should shower first." Bounce. "Ran just before you got here." I never would have known.

"You look fine," I said and meant it.

"No, I don't."

"Yes, you do."

"No, I don't. But if you're really in a hurry I guess we can go now. Let's take my truck and put the dog in the back."

"No, Fritzy. Jennifer would definitely not be okay with being in the back of a truck."

"Why not?" It was as though I'd just said eggnog was bad for your health (which it was, by the way). "Dogs love the wind in their face."

"We'll take my car. She—he—can sit in the back." Missy was getting to me.

"Have it your way." Throw. Swish. "Just one more thing. I was thinking since I was the one who got the business and all . . ." Bounce. "Maybe I should get a finder's fee or something?" She looked at me with enough uncertainty I knew she felt a little awkward in asking. But just a little. "I mean, I really had to sell to her. You would have been proud of me." Bounce. Throw. Swish.

"What did you have in mind?"

"I dunno. What were you thinking?"

"I wasn't thinking. You're the one who brought it up."

"Okay, well then let's say two months of whatever you charge her."

"Two months?"

"You asked what I was thinking, and I asked what you were thinking. I gave you the chance to say it, but you wanted me to say it first, so that's what I was thinking."

"How about two weeks?"

"A month, and I'll cover for you if you ever legitimately need coverage for her."

"Deal." I stuck out my hand and Fritzy crushed it enthusiastically.

"You know what, Wheeler? I think we'd be good business partners. Maybe after we graduate from college we can start a business together."

"I don't want to go into business," I said. "I want to be a graphic novelist."

"Yeah, but maybe until you get famous. Or I could be your agent or something."

"Yeah, maybe. But first things first. Let's go."

I knew I hadn't struck a great deal, but I needed the money. Mom happily accepted my rent money each month so she wasn't going to back down on that. I barely had enough left over for gas and maybe a little bit of fun.

> > >

Liza Dupont was a sweet old lady, and she did insist that we call her "Liza." She was happy to see Fritzy. Happy that Fritzy remembered to come by and introduce my services to her. She was crazy for Jennifer, wondering how I'd ever gotten her to be that lovely shade of pink.

She seemed so unsteady and walked so slowly with the assistance of a cane, I wondered how she ever made it to the library in the first place. I was surprised to learn she still had her driver's license even though she said she didn't feel all that comfortable driving anymore.

"What can you do for me?" she asked after I quoted my price.

"Well, we provide coverage twenty-four-seven for any event that might fall just below the level of an emergency," I rattled off the usual. And, as usual, it failed to impress.

Fritzy, seeing her finder's fee disappear before her eyes, piped in. "You won't regret it, Liza. My neighbor uses Distress Dial, and Hudson's always over there for one thing or another."

She didn't mention I was usually over there to see her, and I sometimes knocked on Pirkle's door just to say Hi, and make him feel like he was getting his money's worth. He usually didn't invite me in, but there had been another strange late-night call recently that I, again, attributed to butt-dialing. Another call where I tried talking to him but got no response and just heard vague mumblings and background noises. I'd gone over the next day and told him to not carry the phone in his back pocket or lie down on top of it, but he just looked at me strangely like he didn't know what I was talking about.

"I'll tell you what, kids," Liza said. "It's a joy just seeing your beautiful young faces today. There are days that go by, and I mean many days, where I don't see a soul except maybe the mailman, and that's only if I time things just right."

Fritzy and I beamed. I suppose we were trying to live up to the beautiful young faces that Liza saw.

"My biggest fear," she went on, "is that I could die in this house and nobody would even know for days or weeks. I never had children of my own. My husband's been gone for twenty years and my sister's children are all the way across the country. They're good about calling, but sometimes a few weeks go by in between calls."

Our smiles disappeared. The idea of dying alone in a house and not being detected for days or weeks . . . well, that was about as dark a concept as either of us could imagine.

"So what can you do for me?" she asked again to our now serious faces.

"You could call anytime you ever feel sick?" Fritzy asked hopefully.

"People my age don't always feel sick before we go," Liza gently informed her. "Often we go without warning."

"I think I have an idea," I said. "How about you call me every day at a certain time? Say six o'clock in the evening. Then, if I don't hear from you by about six fifteen, I'll call you. If you don't pick up the phone, I can come by and check on you. Does that sound like something that would work?"

Fritzy looked at me, and I could see she was

proud of me. I puffed a little higher in my seat. I felt a little older than my age. A daily routine was more than I wanted for a Distress Dial client, but how hard could it be just to answer the phone once a day?

The corners of Liza's eyes crinkled, and a smile spread slowly across her face. For a few seconds I was worried she'd bust out laughing at the absurdity of my suggestion.

"You know what," she said in her crackling little voice, "that's not a half-bad idea. In fact, I think I like it very much."

We sealed the deal with ice cream that Liza insisted on serving. When we finally left and got in the car, Fritzy high-fived me.

"Way to think on your feet, Wheeler," she said.

I pulled out my phone and set a daily alarm for six fifteen.

We were both quiet on the way home. I guess we were thinking the same thing. It was Fritzy who finally put it into words when I pulled up in front of her house.

"You know what? We gotta find a way to get her out of the house more. That's not much of a life she's living." She pushed Jennifer's pink muzzle away from the back of her neck where Jennifer had taken a lick of the free salt left over from Fritzy's run.

"Yeah. I was just thinking the same thing. Or maybe we could take her for a drive every once in a while."

"Okay, let's talk later." Fritzy got out of the car

and walked around to my side, leaning on the roof of the car with one hand. Her face lowered to my level. "You're a good guy," she said. "I'm glad we're friends."

I watched her long, thick braid swing like a pendulum across her strong back as she walked towards the front door. It's funny how girls don't smell bad, I thought. Not even after a sweaty workout.

JENNIFER WAS A BIG HIT...

. . . during his visit. It began with Alana who couldn't get enough of Jennifer and found the mere idea of him to be "irresistible."

"Really, Hudson, he's iconic, don't you think? I mean . . . he's so noble in stature and so perfectly sculpted he's almost hedge-like. And the hot pink in contrast to those qualities. It's like a sociological statement about our culture, like we focus on the flashy external stuff and ignore the real beauty behind it. But also, the flashy is beautiful in its own way. I think we should draw him."

And we did. More than once.

Jennifer was a natural model. It was as if he knew what was expected of him and understood that people's talents were being mobilized in order to memorialize him and everything he stood for, whatever that was.

Alana also decided that Jennifer should star in my graphic novel. A character that changed from white to pink, like Clark Kent to Superman. I still hadn't shared the storyline of my new novel with her, but it was doubtful there'd be a place in the Arctic Circle for a pink poodle. And I wasn't exactly thrilled about other people's ideas creeping into my work.

Alana wanted to come over every day to see Jennifer, whose color I could tell was already fading a little each day. There were pink smudges on the sheets when I came home from school to find Jennifer sprawled across my bed.

One day, Alana asked Penelope and Gus to stop by after school to see Jennifer for themselves.

"Oh my God, the cutest thing ever. You know what I mean?" Penelope turned to Gus who nodded enthusiastically.

"I mean . . .Wow, so awesome. Right? Ha ha ha. Can you believe it?" she said, squealing loudly.

Jennifer, sensing the moment was his, quickly adopted a show dog stance with front and hind legs slightly angled but solidly planted. Head held nobly high and proud.

"So sweet," Gus took up where Penelope left off, his irony escaping her. "Hud, the two of you look so adorable together."

"For real, right?" Penelope gushed. "Pose for a picture."

I didn't.

When they were gone, Alana was upset they'd missed the whole point of Jennifer. The subtle statement he made just by being himself and being that color. She also noticed the lightening of his color, but felt it was better that way. *Nothing of beauty can stay the same forever*, she said. *Or it wouldn't be truly beautiful because beauty was fleeting by nature.*

Me? I thought Alana grew more beautiful every day.

>>>

My last day with Jennifer didn't pass without excitement, although more for him than me. I was home, trying to get a little work done before collecting the dogs for a walk. Jennifer, who always looked forward to hanging out with the group, knew the time was drawing near, so he stood guard by his leash, whining occasionally in case I forgot about The Boys (and Lady). My home phone rang. The land line.

"Hudson?" Mrs. Dickinson always sounded a little nervous when she called, like she expected to be punished for using the service she was paying for.

"Hi, Mrs. Dickinson. What can I do for you?" I tried to kill the sigh in my voice.

"I'm sorry. I know you've told me I'm supposed to use the special phone you gave me, and I'm not supposed to call this number, but the darn thing isn't working again." I heard a loud beep in the background.

"I can take a look when I pick up Lady." A simple

battery charge was sure to be the problem.

"That would be fine, and I'd appreciate it. But I'm calling for another reason, something urgent."

I sat up straight in my bed and Jennifer, sensing the shift in my posture, sprung to his feet and wagged his tail expectantly.

"What's the problem?" The beeping in the background continued.

"My smoke alarm is going off, and I think it's the battery. I was wondering if you could come over and take a look. Lady's just beside herself," she clucked.

It seemed like outside forces conspired to get the dogs walked earlier than planned, so I decided to collect Buster and take him with us. I'd change the smoke alarm battery, leave with Lady, and swing by to pick up Duke. Jennifer was already standing at the sliding glass door that opened onto our backyard where Buster came through the loose board of the fence. That Jennifer was one smart dog.

>>>

"Oh dear, I don't have the right kind." Mrs. Dickinson was riffling through a shoebox full of batteries while I perched at the top of her ladder. "It's the square one, right?"

"The one that looks like this." I passed down the 9-volt, and she inspected it carefully.

"No, I don't have one of those. I'll buy one the next time I go to the market. Would you be able to put it in for me when you come for Lady?"

"No problem." I got off the ladder and folded it up. "At least we got the beeping to stop." I took the ladder back to the pantry.

"Poor Lady." Mrs. Dickinson bent to scratch Lady's head. "Her hearing is so sensitive, you know."

Jennifer, who was very well behaved indoors, stood next to Lady whom he loved. Buster was tied to the leg of a kitchen chair. He couldn't be trusted inside.

"Mrs. Dickinson, is ninety *really* old? I mean . . ." I didn't actually know what I meant by that question. My own grandparents were around seventy, and that seemed *really* old to me. I suppose I wanted to see how Mrs. Dickinson would react to that number. Would she swoon with shock and amazement?

"It depends." She looked frankly at me as though trying to size up what was behind my question. "I know a ninety-five-year-old lady, a lovely lady. There's nothing she can't do. She keeps up with all of us at the Senior Center. Then again, I know people at seventy who are already resigned to the rocking chair, if you know what I mean." I thought I did.

"It all depends on the individual. Their mental well-being. Their physical health. Their desire to persevere. It's not easy getting old, you know?"

"I guess it wouldn't be."

"Why do you ask, Hudson? Is it Len Pirkle?"

"No." I was afraid I'd revealed too much. Mrs. Dickinson was clueless in some ways but pretty sharp in others. "Just curious, I guess."

But she wasn't about to let it go at that. "How is Len these days? Is he still a client of yours? I haven't seen him at the Senior Center in a long while."

"Yes, he's still a client. He's doing just fine."

"Well, you tell him we'd like to see more of him. Men are in high demand at my age. Especially the ones who can still see to drive at night. But you don't have to tell him that last part," she winked.

That was a quality I hadn't considered.

"Mrs. Dickinson. If you don't mind my asking, what do you do at the Senior Center?"

"Why, all kinds of things. We have luncheons just for socializing. We have classes. Computer classes, art classes. Discussion groups on current events. We even have our own library. Stop by sometime and take a look. It's wonderful."

"What if a person is *really* old? I mean, I don't know how old in years but . . . not active the way you are. Would there be something for that person to do at the Senior Center if they could get there?"

"Of course, dear." She put her hands on her hips and gave me that questioning look again. "You're sure we're not talking about Len Pirkle? Because the last time I saw him, he seemed to be in perfectly good health."

"No, not him. I know a lady, another client of mine. She's really nice, but she has trouble getting around, and I don't think she has anything to do during the day. She's always by herself."

"Well, then we must do something about that."

She set down her box of batteries and rummaged through the kitchen drawer for pen and paper. She wrote a few things down and handed the note to me. "You give this to your friend and ask her to call me. I can arrange for the shuttle to pick her up and take her home. Our city taxes pay for these services. They're there to be used."

"I'll do that," I said. "Her name is Liza Dupont. She's really nice, I think you'd like her."

"I'm sure I would. If I don't hear from her in a few days, I'll call on her. You talk it over, and if she's agreeable, just give me her address and I'll pop by."

>>>

Missy and her mother arrived late that night to take Jennifer home. Both owner and dog were overjoyed to see each other, but I have to admit I felt a little dejected. And maybe a little jealous too. Jennifer had become a real pal with an uncanny ability to know what I was going to do even before I knew it myself. It had been nice having him around. Mom, the notorious pet-hater that she was, admitted even she was going to miss him. And Jennifer, a pale salmon-colored shadow of his former self, left behind only the pink stains on my sheets to remind me he was ever there.

DRUG EDUCATION WAS PART OF OUR MIDDLE SCHOOL CURRICULUM...

. . . or rather, *anti*-drug education was. We learned about addiction and how some people can become addicts because the receptors in their brains somehow line up perfectly with the drug (or drink) of choice. Kind of like an electrical plug that only fits into one outlet. Or Cinderella's glass slipper that only fits one foot.

I can't remember a lot about it because I wasn't paying too much attention, but that was the general idea. For a while, I worried about having an outlet in my brain that was a perfect fit for some innocent drug just minding its own business. I'd be walking down the street and . . . ZAP! I'd turn into an addict.

I'd thought about how this same concept could apply to love. What is love, and why does one person fall for another? I mean, really fall, beyond a crush. Beyond lust. It can't be measured objectively, or everyone would be in love with the same person. At times, I've wondered if love was just a matter of being drawn, like a magnet, to the person who will make up for your own inadequacies. Cinderella's slipper in search of a foot. Nothing more than an addiction.

What else explains the absolutely illogical nature of love? Why would a normal-looking girl light up the room for her lover while other, more beautiful women, fade into the background? Why do so many girls want a "bad boy" instead of a nice guy like me? Why does some guy with absolutely no sense of humor triumph over a funny guy (again like me) even though girls are always saying the number one thing they look for in a guy is a sense of humor?

It doesn't make any sense, and I don't know why it happens, but I do know the exact moment I realized I was in love with Alana Love. And I remember how the realization shocked me. And scared me, too. It wasn't at all the pleasant experience I imagined it would be.

>>>

"Look at you." Fritzy nudged me with her elbow, nearly pushing me over even though we were sitting down. "Who would've thought?"

We were two games into the league, and I could safely say I hadn't yet embarrassed myself. Our team consisted of three girls and two guys (myself included). Our fifteen minutes of post-game team camaraderie was over, leaving just Fritzy and me sitting on the hood of her truck, basking in the cool autumn sun and the glow of our win.

"You did good," she said. "The others respect you."

"That's because I'm part of a package that includes you."

"That may be true for now." Fritzy didn't deny it like I was hoping she would. "But the more you play, the better you'll get and people will judge you on your own merits."

"Gee, thanks Fritzy."

"What?"

"I just didn't expect you to agree with me."

"Well, then why did you say it?"

"Never mind. You're so . . . literal."

"Oooh, I'm offended." She tickled me in the ribs, and I jumped off the truck. "C'mon Hudson, if you want a compliment, just ask me. I'll compliment you."

"What're you doing for the rest of the weekend?" I changed the subject.

"Date tonight. Frankie's concert tomorrow, don't forget."

Frankie was the only one Fritzy addressed by first name (actually his middle name). I suppose that's because, being her brother, they shared a last name, and it would just get too confusing.

"I know. I'll be there."

"What about you?" she asked.

"Working on my college applications."

"Right down to the deadline. How many are you submitting? Just the two?"

"That was the agreement with my mom."

"Are you still set on not going?"

"That's the plan."

"You're crazy, Wheeler. Just sayin'."

"And why is that?"

"The whole world is going to pass you by while you're sitting around doing nothing."

"Traveling around the world and writing a novel is doing nothing in your world I suppose?"

Fritzy leaned back against the windshield of her truck and closed her eyes against the weak November sun. She didn't answer, which I knew was her infuriating way of concurring with my last statement.

"Maybe you're the one who'll be doing nothing while the world passes you by," I said. "In your little world of high school on steroids."

"College is not high school on steroids, Wheeler." She didn't move from her reclined sunbathing position as I strutted furiously around the truck.

"And you know that how?"

"It's just not. That's how I know."

"Good answer."

There we went again. I swear we must have been siblings in a past life; we fell into this squabbling so naturally.

"So, you're still planning on accompanying Tat Girl on her travels around the world?"

"Don't call her that."

"Why not? You're the one who told me about the tattoo."

"It's demeaning. She has a name. And I told you because I thought you were my friend."

"I *am* your friend." Her voice rose just enough to tell me I'd hit a sore spot. I was getting through to her. She sat up and swung her legs over the side of the truck. That confirmed it. "Your friends are the ones who are going to tell you the truth. No one else gives a shit."

"I'm just saying, don't call her 'Tat Girl.' I hate it when you do that."

"Then tell me her last name."

"Love."

"You're kidding, right?"

"I'm not kidding."

"Okay, Wheeler, here's what I really think. I think you're an idiot for chasing after Love when she obviously doesn't feel the same about you." That stung. "To me, she sounds a little nutty, forget about the tats. She's dating the quarterback of your football team and refuses to watch him play. She's talked you into following her around the world and giving up on college."

"She didn't talk me into giving up on college. I decided that before I knew her. And I'm not giving up. I choose not to go."

"Well, whatever. You're definitely not going to college now, even if you wanted to change your mind."

"So, your idea of nutty is someone who doesn't like football and doesn't want to go to college. That eliminates more than half the world right there."

"Okay, Wheeler, you win. I'm not getting anywhere with you when it comes to Love, I can see that. I'd say you were pussy-whipped, but you're not even getting any."

"Shut up." I threw the ball at her, but with lighting quick reflexes she snatched it out of the air and threw it back at me, twice as hard. I climbed back on the hood of the truck, shoulder to shoulder with her.

"I meant to tell you . . ." Fritzy began. She had the admirable ability to move on without a trace of hard feelings. "I woke up last night at about three o'clock and went down to the kitchen to get a drink. I looked out the window and saw Pirkle's house all lit up. Every single light in the house must have been on. I almost texted you."

"He does that," I said. "I don't know why. Maybe he gets up and reads or watches TV or something. Maybe he doesn't like the dark."

"What's that on your leg?" she cried out. I looked down quickly, expecting to swat away a yellow jacket or worse. "Oh my God, don't tell me! It's a muscle."

I glanced down at the part of my leg just above my knee to confirm the muscles I'd recently noticed were starting to assert themselves visibly. I flexed my foot to make them pop. Muscles. Such a new concept.

Fritzy pulled up to the curb in front of my house

to drop me off. I grabbed the towel I was sitting on and twisted around to get my gym bag from the backseat.

"Well, what do you know? Love has arrived," Fritzy said. "Is that her?"

I swung around and saw Alana sitting in the shadow of my front doorstep. I was surprised to see her since Saturday wasn't a day she normally spent with me.

"Yeah, that's her." I opened the truck door, feeling my heartbeat accelerating.

"Maybe she has paranormal powers and knew we were talking about her," Fritzy's voice was nothing if not loud. I shushed her as politely as I could.

"I'll see you tomorrow. Text me directions to the concert." I practically fell over myself in my hurry to get out of the truck.

Fritzy took off without another word. I knew I'd hear about it the next time we spoke, the way I shushed her and all. But at the moment, I was only thinking about Alana and her sudden unexpected appearance.

Alana lifted her eyes to me as I walked towards the door, my gym bag slung across my back, a stupid grin pasted across my face. She wore a translucent blue top that dropped below the level of her left shoulder. Her eyes were pools of wonder, her expression soft and inviting. Her lips parted in a smile I was sure could melt the hardest of hearts. Without even knowing what had changed between us, I knew I was in love.

HERE'S A HORROR STORY ...

. . . it goes like this:

The old house sits on the corner of a street like any other street, unremarkable in every way. Nobody pays much attention to what's going on inside the house. Nobody knows who lives there. People walk by every day on their way to work or shopping or dropping off the kids at school, but they're consumed by the petty problems that fill their days and the fantasies that play out in their dreams at night. No one bothers with the old house on the corner.

One day a passerby hears a scream coming from inside, but then he's not sure if it really came from the house or if it was just the squealing tires of a speeding car off in the distance. A few days later, a jogger hops over some splintered shards of glass on the sidewalk and notices a broken window. She jogs off, her thoughts already turning to other more pressing matters. Someone else, a neighbor, thinks he smells smoke coming from the house, and this gets his attention. But when he steps outside to sniff the air, he decides it's probably just a barbecue, although he can't remember ever seeing anyone in the house before. Eventually, the grass in front turns brown from lack of water. The paint peels off in long strips. It becomes obvious the house has fallen into a total state of disrepair that's hard to ignore.

And then one morning, the front door has been left open. The people who live and walk in this neighborhood gather out front, until one brave soul agrees to go inside and see what happened. What he encounters, upon entering, is horrifying. Terrifying chaos. Madness and mayhem.

"Why didn't we see the signs?" the people ask themselves much later. "They were right there in front of us the whole time."

> > >

"Hey, what's up?" Coming across Alana so unexpectedly. On my doorstep. On a Saturday.

"Hi," she stood up and slung her canvas bag over her shoulder. "You doing anything today?"

"Nope. No plans yet."

"Can we hang out?"

"Sure. What's wrong? You seem kind of sad." I unlocked the door and let us in.

"Bryce, what else? We had another fight." She

followed me into the living room where she flopped down on her favorite chair. Being as sweaty as I was, I remained standing.

"Hawaii again?"

"Yup. I don't understand how he can do this to me. It's so blatantly unfair, and he doesn't even see it that way."

I wasn't in the mood to talk about Bryce. Truth is, I was never in the mood to talk about him. To me, the solution was simple. Break up with Bryce and be done with your pain. Move on to someone who appreciates you. Who won't ever let you down. Who loves you. *Woah!*

"Well, I guess you'll have to figure that one out," was all I could say.

"Who was that girl in the truck? Why are you so sweaty?"

"She's just a friend. Lives across the street from one of my clients."

"That big girl who came to your birthday party? Penelope told me about her."

"Yeah, that's her."

"What's her name again? Something weird."

"Fritzy."

"Fritzy," she chuckled. "Cool name. So why are you so sweaty?"

I couldn't tell Alana about basketball and all the training I'd been doing with Fritzy. I couldn't tell her about the basketball league. I wasn't sure if she'd laugh or maybe she'd just think that was something "people like us" didn't do. She hadn't noticed my new muscles. Too subtle.

"Just running around," I said. "I'm going to take a shower. Be right back."

"Hurry. I have something to show you."

>>>

When I came out of the shower, Alana had spread ten sheets of drawing paper across the living room floor.

"Tah-dah!" She stepped aside so I could see. "You inspired me. I've been working on a graphic novel, and I wanted to wait until I had enough material to show you. Do you like it?"

The artwork was good. The story seemed intensely personal, having to do with a relationship spiraling into the depths of relationship hell. In the corner of each panel she drew a poodle, hovering over the action like a guardian angel. The first poodle was hot pink, but it faded with each consecutive drawing until, in the end, it was snow white.

I thought of my Arctic Circle story. It wasn't at all personal, and it showed in the work. Ironically, Alana's story, which wasn't the kind of thing I'd ever read, was probably the kind of thing publishers would drool over. I wanted to feel flattered that I inspired Alana, but all I could feel was resentful. Why did she have to write a graphic novel? That was supposed to be the one thing I could do to shine for her. I was busy with old people and dogs and girls who didn't want me and sports I'd never excel in. And the stuff I was really good at . . . well, that was going nowhere.

"I'm embarrassed to show it to you because you're so talented," she said hesitantly, as though trying to pierce the armor of my blank stare. "And I hope you don't mind I used the pink poodle idea. I know we talked about *you* using it, so I can take it out if you want."

"No, it's great. Really . . . wonderful. I can't believe you've gotten so far with it."

She relaxed after that. "I was wondering if you could help me with a few of the problems." So we worked on her drawings together until Mom came home and invited her to stay for dinner.

There was a constant flow of texts between Alana and Bryce the entire time. As the night went on and we finished washing dishes, she deflated a little with each incoming text.

"Put your phone away, and forget about him for a while." I couldn't take it anymore. "Or just go be with him if you're going to text all night." I knew I sounded sulky, but she was paying more attention to the guy who wasn't in the room than the guy who was.

"I'm sorry, you're right." She dumped her phone into the canvas bag and then pulled it back out and powered it off. "There."

"You wanna do something?" I asked. It was getting kind of late to do anything by then. "You want mc to take you home?"

"Could I stay here tonight?" she asked apologetically. "My dad's traveling, and I don't feel like being alone."

Mom was in her room reading, and I knew I'd have to run it by her, but I also knew she'd probably be fine with it.

"Of course," Mom said when I went into her bedroom to let her know. "Let me get some sheets and I'll make up the sofa for her. Or you can give her your bed and you can take the sofa."

"Just give me the sheets. I'll take care of it. You stay here." I didn't want Mommy tucking us in.

We made up the sofa and Alana said she'd sleep there.

"I'm not going to kick you out of your own bed, Hudson. This is so great, thanks."

We were both tired (me from my basketball workout and her from Bryce-related-depression) so we went to sleep not long afterwards. But sometime in the middle of the night, Alana came into my room and lay down beside me.

"I was lonely," she whispered when I startled awake. "Can I sleep next to you?"

Of course I didn't object.

But nothing happened except that Alana went right to sleep, and I remained wide awake for the rest of the night, not daring to move or even breathe loudly for fear of waking her. Sometime around five in the morning, I crept out of the room, closing the door quietly behind me. I lay down on the sofa and instantly fell asleep. Didn't want Mom to wake up and find us in the same bed.

Mom shook me awake around noon, knowing I was going to Frankie's recital which started at one o'clock. I jumped up and showered while she shook Alana awake. Not realizing I'd spent much of the night in bed with Alana, Mom thought I'd be too embarrassed and modest to go in there and wake her myself.

"Hudson," Alana mumbled groggily before focusing on my mother's hovering face. "Oh, sorry, Mrs. Wheeler."

"Hudson's in the shower because he has to be somewhere in forty-five minutes. I left some sweet rolls out for you kids. He can drop you off on his way, but I have to leave right now."

"Thanks, Mrs. Wheeler. Thanks for letting me stay last night."

"Anytime, honey." And then an unexpected kiss from Mom on the top of Alana's head. I know because Alana told me. Embarrassing, but sweet, I guess, at the same time.

Alana pressed me all the way to her house for more information on my one o'clock date. "A piano recital with the big girl, what was her name . . . Fritzy?"

"Yup."

"What's going on between you two?"

"Nothing."

"I didn't know you liked piano."

"I've started to."

"Are you spending all day with her?"

"I'm not sure how long the recital lasts. There's a reception afterwards I think."

I liked being interrogated by Alana—payback. It gave me a taste for what it feels like to be the object of someone's jealousy, even though I knew it was only friend jealousy and not boyfriend jealousy.

>>>

A piano recital is not as much fun as it sounds. Especially when most of the performers are between the ages of eight and ten. Frankie was clearly Mr. Scolari's star pupil, and I did feel a sort of proprietary pride when he played.

Afterwards, there were refreshments that one of the parents laid out on a table in the back. Surrounded by the members of the Fritz family, I felt like a chihuahua in a pack of Great Danes.

Mr. Scolari came over to congratulate Frankie on his performance. With his dark hair and small stature, he could easily be mistaken for my father. The taut muscles on his forearms quivered when he reached out to shake my hand. His powerful grip didn't fit with the soft melodies that poured out from his fingers.

"Nice to see you here, Hudson," he said. "Thanks for coming out to support us today."

"Wheeler wants to take piano lessons," Frankie blurted out. I was surprised he remembered the one time I'd casually mentioned it, more as a way of trying to bond with him.

"Wonderful!"

I wondered if Mr. Scolari could sense my complete lack of musical ability and enthusiasm.

"One day, but not yet. Maybe after I graduate and save up some money for lessons."

"I hope you'll come to me when you're ready," he said. "I give adult lessons during the day and on weekends. Do you have a piano at home?"

"No."

"You can rent one," Fritzy said. "They're not expensive. And Mr. Scolari comes to your house which makes it a lot easier."

"You're hired!" he laughed. "You're a wonderful salesperson, Lauren. And I know you do a lot to support your brother."

"Yeah, right!" Frankie spat out the most emotional display of wordage I'd ever heard from him. Fritzy reached over and cuffed him on the upper arm. Her version of a love tap.

It had been an eventful weekend, so I had trouble getting to sleep that night. As tired as I was, thoughts of Alana came hurtling at me like a meteor shower. I'd kind of gone to the next level with her even if she hadn't gone there with me. I thought back on the night before and visualized her padding into my room on bare feet. For one dream-second when she had first sat on the side of my mattress, I'd thought it was Jennifer and stretched out my leg to shove him off the bed. But it wasn't Jennifer or even a vision of Alana visiting in my dreams. It was the real live Alana lying next to me. We hadn't snuggled or anything close to it, but her bare leg brushed against mine. Her soft breath whispered over the hairs of my arm, stiffening them and other body parts to total attention.

I wanted her so badly, but I didn't want to want her. It was futile and frustrating. As much as I fantasized about stealing her away from Bryce, I couldn't make myself believe that was possible. And there was the other part. I didn't want to steal her away from anyone. I just wanted her to want me the same way I wanted her. That's why I was already disappointed in love, as new as I was to it. And Alana was disappointed in love as well, but for entirely different reasons. In a strange way, we were bonded together by our disenchantment.

After hours of floating between wakefulness and sleep, awful because it was neither, the ring of my phone was a relief. Too many times my breath had caught with the expectation of a late night phone call from Alana, only to be confronted by Mr. Pirkle's number instead. This time, even though I was prepared, the optimist in me argued for the nanosecond it took me to pick up the phone: *She's thinking of me too. She can't sleep either. We spent the night together last night. She was jealous when she knew I was going to the concert with Fritzy.*

Pirkle's number flashed on my phone screen.

"Hello, Mr. Pirkle," I spoke to what I assumed

would be no one on the other end. I expected the usual whooshings and knocking-about sounds a live phone makes in someone's pocket. But this time was different.

"Come quickly. I can see her." He spoke in a loud, urgent whisper.

"See who, Mr. Pirkle?"

"You already know. I've told you again and again, but you still won't believe me."

"Told me what?"

"Again and again."

"Mr. Pirkle?"

"What's it going to take for you to believe me?" he roared into the phone so loud I had to pull it away from my ear.

"I'm not sure I understand what you're saying."

"I'm saying come quickly! How much clearer can I get?"

"Are you sick?"

"Of course I'm not sick!"

Click

Dead silence.

What the hell? Is he crazy? Should I call the police? He's old, but he's probably still strong enough to kill me. Should I wake up Fritzy and tell her I'm going over there? My thoughts raced.

And then after a few minutes . . . *Grow a pair, Hudson.*

I scrambled out of bed and threw on some clothes. It actually felt good to end the pretense of sleep and get up and do something. I scratched out a quick note for Mom and left it on my bed in the unlikely event she'd come into my room at this hour.

When I arrived at Pirkle's house, it was all lit up like before. I saw his face peering out the window of his second-floor bedroom, but then it disappeared. I know he saw me. I walked to the front door and put my ear against it for a second. I heard heavy footsteps which I knew came from the stairway that ended only feet away from the door. I knocked and waited. No more footsteps, and no answer. I rang the doorbell and waited. Receding footsteps this time but still no answer.

I was about to turn around and get back in my car and go home, but I remembered the key. Pirkle had shown me where he hid it in the backyard in case I ever needed it in the event of an emergency. Questions littered my brain. *Was this an emergency? And if so, why not just call the cops?* But I couldn't bring myself to call the cops, and I couldn't bring myself to leave. I walked around the side of the house and lifted the latch of the gate that led to the backyard. With the bright house lights illuminating my way, I found the key beneath a bush and under a rock. Then I walked back to the front door and rang the doorbell again. Finally, I turned the key and opened the door.

"Mr. Pirkle?" I called out. "It's me, Hudson. I used the emergency key to get in." I tried to come off as confident and casual, but I knew my voice was shaky with fear. I should have let Fritzy know what I was doing. But this was my responsibility, not hers.

>>>

Much later I asked myself why I hadn't seen the signs. They were right there in front of me the whole time.

CAN A PERSON LOOK CONFUSED AND FIERCE ...

. . . at the same time? Strong and weak? Welcoming and hostile? I wouldn't have believed it to be true until that night.

I didn't see Pirkle when I first opened the door. My eyes swept the living room to the right of me and the kitchen to the left. Then I looked at the staircase and saw him standing in the shadow of the landing. He was as still as a statue, naked except his underwear and combat boots. Tightly gripped in his hands, a baseball bat. His hair, normally neatly slicked back, was sticking out every which way. Even his eyebrows jutted from his forehead like battle flags. My stomach churned, and for a second I thought I was going to be sick.

"Mr. Pirkle?"

He didn't say anything. Just continued to look at

me like he was trying to figure out what I was doing there. And then after what seemed like an eternity, he spoke.

"Oh, it's you," he said so softly I almost couldn't hear. "What do you want? Why are you here?"

"You called me."

"You called me?"

"No, *you* called *me*."

Our standoff continued with him about ten steps above me on the landing. Still clutching the bat, although by that point it hung from just one hand.

"I don't think so," he said cautiously.

"I came by to check on you," I tried a different approach.

"Well since you're here, hurry and come upstairs."

"Um . . ."

"Um, what?"

"Why do you have that bat? Is something wrong?"

"Prowler," he said. "I heard a prowler outside. I've been broken into before. This time I'm ready for them."

"It wasn't a prowler, it was just me. I went around the back to get the emergency key when you didn't answer the door."

"Just you then?"

"Yes, sir. Just me."

"Sure about that?" His eyes danced in his head.

"Yes, I'm sure."

"We're wasting time. Come on up."

"Could you put the bat down, please? It's making

me nervous."

He shook his head, visibly annoyed, before leaning the bat up against the corner of the landing. I followed him up the stairs. Trailing behind him, I was close enough to see the power of the muscles in his back, even though the skin was brown and wrinkly like old leather and spotted with tufts of silvery hair. His boots made deep clomping sounds with each step. I felt like I was padding on kitten paws.

"Where are we going?" I asked.

He didn't answer so I just followed him into his bedroom, the only room in the house that was dark. It was the first time I'd been up there, and nothing looked out of the ordinary except for the balled-up bed sheets laying in a pile on the floor. He led me to a window which overlooked his backyard, and I was surprised to see the picture of the little girl propped up on the window ledge. Also on the ledge, a pair of high-powered binoculars which he thrust into my hands.

"Stand here," he instructed. "Keep looking right at that window across the way. The one that's lit."

A house which rose above the fence of his back-yard was like the x-ray opposite version of Mr. Pirkle's. Where his was light, the other was dark. An upstairs window, small and round, shone brightly in the adjacent house, directly opposite from Mr. Pirkle's bedroom. The last thing in the world I wanted to do was spy on his neighbor with those binoculars. It felt way too creepy.

"I don't think we should be doing this." I handed the binoculars back to him. "It's probably illegal or something."

"Illegal? I'll tell you what's illegal. That's my daughter over there."

"Your daughter lives there?"

"Lives, no. But she's there. I just saw her." He tapped on the framed photo of the little girl. "That's her picture. Without a doubt, it's her."

I glanced at the little room across the way but didn't see anybody. I was one hundred percent confused, but I was pretty sure he was even more confused than I was.

"The girl you saw looked like this girl in the picture?"

"That's right. My daughter."

"But your daughter . . . she wouldn't be this age now would she?"

"Three . . . three-and-a-half almost."

"But . . . this picture was taken a long time ago, wasn't it?"

"A long time ago?" For a second something seemed to click but then he went on. "Keep looking. She'll be back any minute."

It occurred to me there wasn't a hint of alcohol on Pirkle's breath.

"Can I bring a chair over here?" I asked. "So I can sit down."

"Go ahead." He stared out the window towards the tiny circle of light.

I dragged the chair over to the window and sat down. Pirkle continued to stand, occasionally bringing the binoculars up to his eyes. From time to time, I'd glance guiltily at the window but never saw so much as a shadow. Ten, fifteen minutes went by. I yawned. He yawned in response.

"Mr. Pirkle?"

"Hmm?"

"Should I tell you a story?" It worked the last time, and I was pretty tired in spite of all the adrenaline pumping through my veins.

"A story? Do you know a good one?" he muttered, still focused on the neighbor's window.

For some reason, I realized he probably didn't remember my last story. Not in his current state. I thought I'd give it a try. He liked it before.

"Did I ever tell you the story about when my father promised to buy me a car?"

"No. I don't think so." He put the binoculars down on the window ledge, walked over to the side of his bed, and sat facing me.

"I was around seven years old, and my father was about to go away for a long time," I began.

By the end of the story, Pirkle was looking at me in that familiar head-ducking way, and I knew he was back. The real Pirkle, not the weird, nearly naked one.

"Military?" he asked. "Your dad?"

"Yes, sir. Army. He was killed in Iraq."

"It's a real shame, Hudson. A real shame." He lay back on his bed, combat boots and all. "You know, I was a military man myself. Marines."

"Really? Did you fight in World War II?"

"Yes, I did. The Pacific front. We fought over every last God-forsaken scrap of coral in that whole goddamn ocean. I thought it would never end. But it did. Eventually everything does."

His voice showed signs of fatigue, and when he finally threw his head back on the pillow, he let loose with a series of rip-roaring snores. I sat in the dark watching him for about five minutes until it didn't seem like he was going to wake up. How he slept through that, I couldn't imagine.

I glanced over at the circular window again. The light was off, but I'd seen no one. I stood up and walked to the side of his bed where I picked up one of the blankets from the floor and shook it out. Couldn't be too comfortable sleeping in those boots, but I didn't want to risk waking him by pulling them off. I covered him with the blanket and walked down the stairs and out the door, locking it behind me with the emergency key which I slipped into my pocket. I'd return it the next time I was there.

I looked up at the sky full of stars, dimmed slightly by the brightness of Pirkle's house. Home. School. Alana. They were worlds away.

HOW LONG CAN A PERSON SURVIVE . . .

. . . without sleep? I flagged Mom down before she left for work the next morning and asked if we could meet for lunch. She was so pleased, I felt a little guilty it wasn't a spontaneous show of filial affection. I needed information. And sleep.

I dragged myself through yoga, even nodding off during our sustained stretching poses.

"What's wrong with you?" Alana asked at passing period. "You look like a zombie."

"I'm tired. Didn't get much sleep last night. Work." It was tough stringing words together for even the simplest sentence.

After art, I went straight home and fell into bed praying the phone wouldn't ring. I doubt I'd have heard it if it did. When my alarm went off twenty minutes before Mom's lunch break, I was sleeping so soundly I had a moment of total confusion upon waking. Which made me think of Pirkle and the time he thought he was in his old house.

>>>

I like eating in the hospital cafeteria, which most people find strange. There are the usual sad and worried faces of patients' families, but for me, the familiar faces were Mom's co-workers and friends. We picked a small table off in the corner where I could talk to her privately.

"So, my client Mr. Pirkle . . ." I needed to phrase it in just the right way to keep Mom from blowing it out of proportion. She looked at me expectantly. "He's called a few times at night and . . ."

"Did they ever catch the people who burglarized him?" she interrupted.

"No . . . I don't think so. But anyway, he's called a few times at night, and I think those were just butt-dials . . ."

"Butt dials?"

I tried not to sigh.

"You know. When you sit on the phone in your back pocket and it randomly dials a number. My number's programmed into Mr. Pirkle's phone, so it happens."

"I guess it's a good thing I keep mine in my purse."

"It could happen there too. Anyway, once when I was over at his house, he seemed really confused. He said something about how he thought he was at his old house, and I think he was scared and just wanted to talk to someone."

I didn't mention the story about the toy car, and how I'd told it to him. Twice. I wondered if I'd ever be able to tell Mom about that. And if she'd view it as a betrayal that I'd confided in an almost-stranger instead of her.

"Doesn't he have any family or close friends he can talk to?"

"That's just it. I don't think he does. I mean, I know he has a daughter, but I don't know where she is or even if she's alive. She'd be old by now because he's ninety."

"There must be someone."

"Anyway, last night he called, and I went over there, and he was pretty out of it."

"You went over there? What time?"

"You were asleep, and I didn't want to wake you so I left a note."

"Hudson, is this really a good idea? Maybe it's time for you to just get a normal job."

"Can we not talk about that now? Can I just finish what I'm trying to say?"

She looked down at her plate and took a deep breath.

"Okay, I'm sorry. Go on. What do you mean *out of it*? How out of it?" Her eyes narrowed suspiciously.

"Just confused again. Saying stuff like his daughter is living in the neighbor's house and she's three years old. Like that."

"It could be delirium. Or it could be dementia."

"Dementia? No! Talk to him during the day and he's like you and me. I mean . . . he's really sharp."

"Deborah, is this your son?" A young nurse stood at our table. She wore Winnie the Pooh scrubs and had a kind, reassuring face.

"Becky, this is Hudson. Hudson, Becky and I used to work together in the pediatric ward. She still does."

"We had a great time together," Becky smiled. "It was only for a few months, but I really enjoyed working with your mom." She turned to Mom. "He favors you," she winked. "Strong family resemblance."

I barely heard what she said. That word "dementia" was beeping in my head like Mrs. Dickinson's broken smoke alarm. Mr. Pirkle. Imposing. Strong. Dignified. Sometimes gruff, bordering on rude. Demented? No. Demented was like a clown or some character in a horror movie.

"Enjoy your lunch," Becky was saying.

"Thanks for stopping to say hi," Mom kicked me under the table to get my attention.

Dementia? I thought. I just wanted Becky to leave so I could tell Mom how wrong she was. "Nice to meet you."

"How's the pizza?" Mom asked once Becky was gone.

"Mom, he's not demented. I mean, he gets confused. But old people get confused a lot. I mean, sometimes I see it in Mrs. Dickinson. I tell her to restart her computer when she's having a problem and then the next time I have to tell her all over again. And Grandma always forgets where she puts her keys, even though she's not even that old."

"I didn't say he was demented. I said it sounds to me like he might be suffering from dementia. There's a difference between dementia and forgetfulness."

"Like what?"

"Like forgetting where you put your keys or how to fix a broken computer is probably just forgetfulness. Thinking your elderly daughter is three years old. Well, that sounds like dementia."

"But I'm telling you: he's perfectly normal. Even above normal during the day. It's just that I think he gets confused at night. Maybe he's not sleeping well. Maybe he's drinking. When I woke up today I didn't know where I was for a second."

"There's a syndrome called sundowner's," Mom said. "We see it in the hospital in some of our elderly patients. Patients with Alzheimer's and other forms of dementia sometimes get worse when the sun goes down. No one's exactly sure why it happens. Maybe your Mr. Pirkle is suffering from that aspect of it."

My Mr. Pirkle?

"He's fine during the day."

"Hudson, you're not with him every day. You don't know what goes on behind closed doors. And there *are* people who only suffer from sundowner's syndrome. It's a sort of night-time only form of dementia. Less common but it happens."

I put down my second slice of pizza. Suddenly I wasn't hungry.

"Is there anything they can do for it?" I asked. "Any medicine that can cure it?"

"Cure? No. But he needs to see a doctor. You have to call in his support system. You're not equipped to deal with this. You're too young, and you don't have the expertise."

"I told you, there *is* no support system."

"There always is," Mom said. Mom with a support network so vast, she couldn't imagine life without one. "People *like* you, Hudson. They open up to you. Just dig a little."

>>>

It was late by the time I got around to walking the dogs, so it wasn't completely surprising that I ran into Bryce driving Alana home from school. It was embarrassing even though it shouldn't have been. After all, Alana knew it was my job, and she loved the dogs, especially Jennifer. But when it came to a side-by-side, and one guy's taking you home in his brand-new SUV and the other one's walking a bunch of dogs, there was no comparison.

Bryce leaned on the horn right when he got up behind me which made me jump and caused the dogs to lurch forward, straining against their leashes. I didn't fall, but I didn't exactly look graceful either. In her anxiety, Lady ducked between my legs, looping the leash around my ankle. This gave the other dogs the idea to do the same thing which resulted in me assuming the awkward position of hopping on one foot, arms flailing. They pulled up alongside me, and Alana rolled down her window.

"Hey, Hudson. Whatcha doing?"

Bryce leaned over and smiled (smirked?). "Hey, man," he said.

"Hi . . ." I searched for the group in my universe that could include both Alana and Bryce, " . . .guys." I yanked Duke back from the gutter and shook off Lady's leash. "Just walking the dogs," I added foolishly. Of course I was walking the dogs.

"Hi, Jenn-i-fer," Alana puckered her lips in that baby-talk way people do with pets and babies. "His name's Jennifer, but he's a boy," she said to Bryce. She said it to be funny—to bring us together, the two guys in her life. Bryce and I weren't ever going to be buds or hang out, trading compliments about our girl. But maybe we could come together and laugh at a dog's ridiculous name.

It didn't work that way, at least not for me. If anything, it made me feel worse, as if *I* was the one with the girl's name.

"Ha!" he snorted while Alana provided the supportive back-up laughter. "Why's he have a girl's name?"

"I know. Huh?" Alana said. "Bye, Hudson. See you tomorrow."

The window rolled up and off they drove.

I was the guy who walked the dog with a girl's name.

The guy who'd be there for Alana the next day when Bryce was off playing football.

IF YOU NEED TO DIG, A SHOVEL WILL USUALLY DO THE TRICK...

. . . but in Pirkle's case, it took a bulldozer.

I rapped on the door with a sinking sensation, not sure who would be behind it. It'd been three days since the underwear/combat boots incident, and I needed to return the key. And dig.

The man who answered was the dignified Mr. Pirkle. And the reserved Mr. Pirkle. But after our last visit, I wasn't sure I'd be invited in.

"I'm returning the key," I said by way of explanation. "I took it home with me the other night."

"Oh, yes," he said uncertainly dropping the key into his pocket. "Why . . . tell me again why I gave it to you."

"I took it. In case I needed to get in. Do you want me to put it back in the hiding place?"

"Yes . . . no. That's not necessary. I'll do it."

When I didn't leave and the silence extended beyond the normal comfort zone, he invited me in.

"Would you like something to drink, Hudson? I'm afraid all I have is diet soda or water."

"Water's fine." I followed him into the kitchen. "I thought I'd drop by and return the key. I was going to stop by your neighbor's afterwards."

"You sweet on that girl?" Pirkle asked. "I've seen you over there. Seem to be spending a lot of time together."

I thought about the times I'd seen him peering out the front kitchen window when Fritzy and I were shooting hoops. "No, nothing like that," I said. "We're just friends, and we play on a basketball league together." That last sentence came out with feigned indifference, but I was prickly with pride when I said it.

"Pretty girl," he handed me a glass of water. "Should we sit here in the kitchen?"

"Mr. Pirkle, I have another reason for coming." I'd rehearsed this scenario multiple times in the past few days. "I'm doing a project for my government class about WWII, and I wondered if I could interview you about your personal experiences."

He'd never know this wasn't the truth. And what older person could refuse to help a young person working on a school project? This would be my gateway to his mind. Or so I hoped.

"Government class. What docs WWII have to do

with government class?"

I'd actually thought about that too and realized it would have been better to say history class. But I was a terrible liar, and although I was lying about the school project, I couldn't bring myself to lie about the actual class I was taking.

"We're learning about the Department of War and how it ceased to exist right after WWII and eventually became the Department of Defense."

This was the answer I'd fortunately prepared ahead of time even though it still didn't explain where his personal WWII experiences fit in. I was hoping he'd buy it. He gave me the head-ducking, skull-examining look.

"I told you I was a WWII vet?"

"You mentioned it once."

"I don't know how interesting my experiences would be to anyone."

"It would be very interesting to me, if you don't mind."

"I suppose I could answer a few questions," he said cautiously.

I pulled out the folded piece of paper and pen from my back pocket which I'd brought to make it look like I was taking notes for my class. Where to begin? I just wanted to get him talking, hoping something useful might be spilled.

"Were you drafted, or did you enlist?" I began.

"I enlisted," he said. "Before the war. Before Pearl Harbor. My buddy and I. We grew up together, and after high school it seemed like a good idea since we didn't have any other plans. We were working at dead-end jobs, and a lot of us thought that war was coming. Better to enlist and determine your future, than get drafted. Shows you how much we knew."

"What was your friend's name?" The chances of him still being alive were remote, but I kept digging like Mom said.

"His name was Charles, but he went by Chuck."

The "was" made clear that Chuck was past tense. And of course, he didn't volunteer a last name. It would have been strange if I asked for one.

"How did you feel after you enlisted?" *Stupid question.*

"I don't remember. I s'pose I felt all right." *Ask a stupid question, you'll get a stupid answer.*

"Why did you decide to join the Marines?"

"How'd you know I was a Marine?"

"You mentioned it that one time."

He seemed to ponder that before going on.

"Why did I decide to join the Marine Corps? I don't know. It seemed like another good idea. Chuck's father was a Navy man. I suppose that might have influenced his decision, and I went along with it."

"Where did you fight during the war?"

"We fought everywhere. You throw a dart at a map of the Pacific Ocean, and I s'pose we fought there."

"Were you married when you enlisted?" *Here goes!*

"Nope. That came a little later. A gal I met at a

USO dance before we shipped out."

"Was your daughter born after the war?"

"How'd you know about my daughter?"

"You showed me her picture. The little girl with the curly hair." As if I had to remind him who his daughter was. My mouth was dry and my hands were sweaty, anxiety having taken moisture from one body part and redistributed it to another.

"She was born while I was off fighting."

He looked so sad I was almost relieved when he ended the "interview." Almost relieved even though I'd gotten no useful information.

"Hey, I bet that gal is waiting for you," he said, and I knew my time was up.

>>>

"I need your help, but I can't tell you why," I said to Fritzy after I left Pirkle's house.

"If you can't tell me why, then why would I help?"

"Why not? I thought we were friends."

"I like to know what I'm getting into, Wheeler."

We sat at her kitchen table, glasses of eggnog in front of us. With Thanksgiving just ahead, I even kept a carton of the stuff in my fridge, in case Fritzy ever stopped by. Mom wasn't big on it.

"It has to do with client confidentiality," I said. "And if I told you, I'd be breaking the unspoken rule."

"Pirkle?" she asked, one eyebrow shooting up.

"Client confidentiality," I repeated.

"If it's an unspoken rule, then it doesn't really

exist. Besides, I'm almost part of your business, with our agreement about Liza and all."

"I guess." I wiped away my eggnog moustache with a paper towel. "I guess you're kind of an employee in a way."

"Employee? More like I'm like a part owner."

"Part owner? Excuse me? Just because you brought in a piece of business, which by the way I paid you for . . ."

"And I'm on call if you ever can't get to Liza."

"And also by the way, you said you were going to take her for a drive."

"Which I did last weekend. And you said you were going to hook her up with the Senior Center."

"She didn't want to go. Mrs. Dickinson had it all arranged, but the day she was supposed to go, she called and told me it wasn't her thing—hanging around a bunch of old people."

"A bunch of old people? What does she think *she* is? She'd rather be alone with her once-a-day phone calls to you? That's pathetic."

"I put a lot of effort into those calls. She looks forward to them."

"Anyway, what's the big secret, Wheeler? Enough with the bullshit. Spill it."

And I did.

The little girl in the picture with the curly hair. The nighttime phone calls, one of which Fritzy had been present for. The so-called burglary, if it was even that. The confusion about what house he was in. The combat boots and underwear. Mom's unofficial diagnosis of dementia. The girl in the window of his neighbor's house. I felt disloyal for revealing the information, but I trusted Fritzy to keep it to herself. She wasn't a gossiper.

"Don't tell anyone," I said when it was over. "You're bound by client confidentiality too."

"Don't worry. What do you take me for?"

"I'm not worried. Just needed to say that. So we're good with everything, right?"

"What are you going to do about it?" she asked. "Are you going to turn him in?"

"Turn him in for what? It's not like he committed a crime or anything. I'm just trying to find out if there's someone who can step in to help. Family or close friends."

"And?"

"So far, I haven't been able to find out anything. It's like he has no one. Or at least nobody he wants to tell me about. But I'll keep trying."

"I never see anyone go over there." Fritzy put down the empty glass and belched. I must have grimaced because she looked right at me and belched again. "I'll watch out for any unusual activity. It's like that movie where the kid's spying on his neighbor who turns out to be a killer."

"Slow down. Pirkle's not a killer, and we're not in a movie."

"So, what do you want from me?" she asked.

"I was wondering if you know the people in the

house that backs up to his. And if you know anything about the little girl who lives there. Maybe I could have the parents bring her by to prove to him she's not his daughter. Or at least I could be ready if it ever happens again. I'd know what to say to him."

"I know some of the people in the neighborhood. I used to have a paper route when I was younger. Show me which house you're talking about."

We walked around the block until we got to the street behind Pirkle's. Then we counted back until we were at the house which would have been directly facing his backyard. I recognized the brown shingles and steeply-sloped roof. The front yard was unassuming. Manicured hedges lining the sidewalk. Flower beds along the walkway leading up to the front door. A few ordinary-looking trees here and there. No sign of kids' toys or tricycles.

Fritzy stopped in front of the house, hands on hips, and gave the house a once-over.

"Congratulations, Wheeler, this is Scolari's house you were spying on. You peeping Tom."

"Scolari?"

"Your future piano teacher."

"Woah! I guess it's good we know him. That'll make it easier to explain to Pirkle if it happens again. How old is his daughter?"

My gaze strayed to the second floor.

"He doesn't have any kids," Fritzy said. "He moved here a few years ago, and he doesn't even have a wife or a girlfriend that I know of. Wanna go for our run now?"

PEOPLE USUALLY TAKE THE PATH OF LEAST RESISTANCE...

. . . which often translates to wishful thinking. At least, it did for me.

Days disappeared, one behind the other, and suddenly I was looking at Thanksgiving weekend—four days of homework catch-up, family turkey feast at my aunt and uncle's, and a youth group retreat which was so far removed from anything I'd ever do on my own, but I was going as Fritzy's guest.

I loved the whole holiday season starting with Thanksgiving and finishing with New Year's Day which signified the beginning of the end-of-school-year countdown. But this year I thought about it in a different way. Mrs. Dickinson would be flying to Chicago where her daughter lived, and Lady was coming to stay with me for the long weekend. But as far as I knew, Liza and Mr. Pirkle would be alone. That took a little of the glow off that warm feeling I usually carried around inside of me that time of year.

Speaking of Pirkle, it had been five days since I spoke to him, and the idea of reaching out and digging slipped a few notches on my priority list. I was going to do it. It was still important. It still really bothered me when I allowed myself to think about it, so I just didn't allow myself to think about it too much. Then that Wednesday before Thanksgiving, something was bothering Alana during yoga class, and I knew I'd hear about it during passing period. Hoping it was bad news about Bryce, I ditched Gus in the locker room, knowing Penelope would wait for him.

"What are you doing this weekend?" Alana asked. The mope in her voice was audible.

"We're going to my uncle's for Thanksgiving. But I'll be around except for Sunday."

"What's happening Sunday?" she asked like a jealous wife.

"I'm going to a youth retreat with a friend."

"What friend?" Alana knew me well enough by then to know I only had a handful of meaningful friends.

"Fritzy," I answered, wondering why I should feel guilty about it.

"The big girl?"

"Yes, the big girl, Alana. You know who Fritzy is, so you don't have to say that every time I mention her name."

She looked down, and when she looked up again, I saw her eyes were soft with the shine of tears.

"I didn't mean anything by it." She had that nasally snotty sound when she spoke like she was holding back a floodgate. "Seems like you're a little touchy about her."

"Okay, sorry for jumping on you. So what are you doing for Thanksgiving?"

"My dad and I are going to the restaurant at the Hilton on Thursday. They serve a Thanksgiving dinner."

"That sounds like fun," I lied. It sounded like the most depressing thing I could imagine, but I couldn't invite people to my uncle's house.

"Guess what Bryce's doing?"

"Um . . . do I have to?"

She ignored my sarcasm. "He's going with his family to their house in Palm Springs."

"Cool. Must be nice to have a house in Palm Springs."

"He didn't invite me."

"Oh. Well, sorry about that."

I didn't care. I didn't care. And yet, I so cared about her unhappiness.

"I didn't really expect him to. I mean, we hardly ever spend any time at *his* house. With his family. But . . . it just hurts, you know?" Her nasally, snotty cry-voice got all quivery.

I wanted to reach over and grab her hand and

squeeze it, or put my arm around her shoulder and draw her close to me, or tousle her messy hair and tell her everything would be all right. But I couldn't touch her that way. Those were our unspoken rules.

"I'm sorry," was all I said.

"Thanks." We'd reached the door to art class. "Hudson . . . I decided I'm going to see my mother this weekend. I'm going to leave Friday and come back Sunday."

"Your *mother*?" She hardly ever talked about her mother, and I certainly didn't know her mother was within visiting distance. "Where does she live?"

"In the foothills . . . gold country. It's about a four-hour drive from here. I haven't seen her in over a year."

"Are you going with your dad?"

"Are you kidding? My dad doesn't want anything to do with her. But he doesn't care if I go. He actually wants me to visit her more often than I do."

"So how are you getting there?" I knew Alana didn't have a driver's license, and Bryce was going to Palm Springs.

"There's a Greyhound Bus that goes there. It takes a lot longer, about seven hours each way, but it's fine, I've done it before."

"Seven hours? You'll practically just get there and have to turn around."

Could I see the trap being set for me? No. Eighteen-and-in-love equaled "stupid."

"It's fine." Her thick lashes were dewy with

tears. "It's something I have to do even though I'm completely freaked out by the idea. But I know it's probably the last time I'll see her for . . .whenever . . . a long time. I mean, if I go . . . if *we* go traveling after graduation, I don't know when I'll be back. I don't know if I'll *ever* want to live in this country again."

The trap was set and had already been sprung. I was already thinking about how I was going to get out of the retreat with Fritzy. Who was going to take care of Lady? Who was going to cover for Distress Dial calls? How was I going to catch up on homework?

Sometimes, even now, I wonder why I stuck around hoping for as long as I did when it was obvious to everyone, including me, I didn't stand a chance. The answer is, undoubtedly, that my addiction to her was so strong I was willing to accept her on any terms, even if it was much less than what I needed. And there was always the hope I'd be the last man standing and win her love through sheer perseverance.

>>>

Mom was furious. I didn't expect her to be happy, but I didn't think she'd be *that* mad.

"Who's supposed to watch the dog? I hope you're not thinking I'm going to do it. Who's going to take your business calls if they come in? Again . . . not me."

"I'll take care of it, Mom. Don't worry. You don't

have to do anything."

"And you're going to take care of it, how?"

"Fritzy's my business partner," I lied. If Fritzy could only hear me throwing that out so easily after we'd just argued about it. "She'll step up. It's just for three days."

"She's going to take the dog into her home?"

I hadn't asked Fritzy, but I was counting on it. Without her, the trip couldn't happen. I also hadn't told her I wouldn't be going to the youth retreat.

"She'll do everything. It's fine. The business is on auto-pilot."

"Auto-pilot? Last I remember your Mr. Pirkle was in the middle of a meltdown. So you're going to saddle Fritzy with that responsibility just to give Alana a ride which, by the way, I hope she's at least paying for gas."

Hearing her talk about Pirkle's meltdown made me flinch. I'd been pretty good at burying that somewhere in the dark recesses of my mind for the past week. Hearing Mom put it that way made me think about the gerbils I got when I was twelve. I'd begged Mom for a pet when the goldfish wasn't quite cutting it. She didn't want to deal with a cat or a dog so we agreed on a gerbil—actually two. They were fun at first but soon started fighting. Every morning I'd wake up and check on them only to find one or the other bloodied. My duty to the gerbils quickly evolved from pleasure to ball and chain. Why had I asked for them? Finally, I convinced Mom we needed to return them to the pet store. I wasn't equipped to handle the devastation that occurred inside their cage on a daily basis. I never asked for another pet again.

When I first started my business, I didn't think of it as a ball and chain. But that was before Alana Love came into my life.

"She'll pay, Mom. Her dad gives her all the money she needs. She has her own credit card."

Mom stood before me, hands folded across her chest, casting the evilest eye she could muster in my direction. I knew it was almost over.

"Isn't that nice for her?" she dripped sarcasm. "Okay, Hudson. You're eighteen and you're obviously going to do what you're going to do. Since you're an adult, behave like one and drive responsibly."

>>>

Fritzy didn't yell at me like my mom did. But then again, she didn't have to. Fritzy was pretty good at conveying her feelings with the arch of a disapproving eyebrow or the curl of a skeptical lip.

"You're going to owe me big time, Wheeler," she said.

She wasn't kidding. When we'd finished negotiating, I'd agreed to pay her the equivalent of one month's Distress Dial profits for being on standby for Pirkle (who probably wouldn't call). I'd keep up my calls to Liza who wouldn't know where I was as long as we had daily contact. Pirkle's calls would come to me and only be routed to Fritzy if he required an actual visit. Even then, Fritzy would only have to walk across the street. She'd get all the money for taking Lady into her home for three days. In addition, I'd owe her one big favor sometime in the future.

"I'm sorry about the youth retreat," I said. "I was really looking forward to it."

"Don't even say that. It just makes you sound stupid."

"I mean it."

"Well then don't go with Alana. It's not like someone's holding a gun to your head."

"If you were in trouble and needed a friend to help you out, wouldn't you want me to be there for you?"

"I *am* being there for you." She flipped her heavy braid from one shoulder to the other.

"I mean Alana. She's having a really tough time with all this. Her mom has practically been non-existent in her life, and it's not easy for her to face it alone. Her dad won't go with her. You don't know what it's like. You have a mom and dad who love you."

Fritzy shook her head in disbelief and then spoke slowly and deliberately. "Wheeler, please spare me the drama. Why are you always making excuses for that girl?"

"I'm not always making excuses."

"You're always making excuses. And you're always getting caught up in her drama. Do you actually think she's going to dump her boyfriend just because you're driving her to see her mother? Think again."

I knew she was right, but I didn't care. I didn't care that I was making a fool of myself. I was about to have three days away from home with just me and Alana. And her mother, of course.

"I . . ."

"Just go, Wheeler. I'll see you when you get back. And don't worry about the retreat, I've got plenty of friends there. Just too bad you're not going to be one of them."

>>>

It was drizzling and gray when we pulled onto the freeway the day after Thanksgiving. With all the negatives weighing on me, the weather was a perfect match for my mood, although Alana's happy chatter slowly chipped away at my wall of doom and gloom. The path of least resistance . . . it was looking pretty good to me right then. But I was committed, and there was no turning back.

As the freeway turned into a smaller freeway which turned into a freeway in name only, I felt a little bit lightened from the heavy load of guilt I'd been carrying around. We drove on country roads through towns that looked like they hadn't had make-overs since the gold rush days. That was a good thing in my mind.

"It's like another world out here." I imagined a life where Alana and I lived on a ranch, grew all our own food, tended a zoo's worth of animals, and wrote graphic novels in our spare time.

"It's pathetic." A bucketful of cold water on the imaginary ranch and all its animals. "I can't believe my mother and sister choose to live out here."

"Wait. Your *sister?*"

"Yeah, my sister lives with my mom."

"You never mentioned you had a sister."

"I didn't? I'm sure I must have. Well, anyway I have a sister . . . Chloe."

"How old is Chloe?"

"Fifteen."

I was astonished. A bad parent is one thing. Okay, I guess I could understand how you avoid seeing them for a year. But a sibling? I'd prayed for a sibling my whole life and felt cheated for not having one. Alana had a sister and chose not to have contact with her? Bizarre.

"How about your dad? Does he ever see Chloe?"

"No, she doesn't want to see him. When the divorce happened it was like battle lines were drawn, and on one side was me and my dad. On the other, my mom and Chloe."

"Sad."

"I don't know about sad. Sad would be if any of us cared and wanted things to be different. But we don't."

"I still think it's sad." We stopped at a red light on one of the main streets of a small town, which was actually a named freeway though you'd never know it. "You wanna stop to use the bathroom or get something to eat?" I asked.

"Nope," Alana answered tersely. Prompted by the tightness in her voice, I looked over at her, but she stared straight ahead. "I don't think it's *sad*, Hudson. I don't need your pity."

"I'm not pitying you. I just meant that I think it's sad when family members don't want to be together, that's all."

"Families are made up of distinct individuals. They don't all march in lock step and they don't always like each other or have anything in common with each other for that matter. We don't get to pick our family members. Don't you ever fight with your mom?"

"Of course I do. But I wouldn't ever cut her out of my life. She's my mom."

"Well, to me, sad is more like when your dad dies when you're ten years old. But you don't hear me saying that, do you?"

I exhaled heavily. I never expected retaliatory pettiness like that from Alana Love.

"Okay, Alana, you're right. I'm a sad case. Now can we move on?"

The car behind us honked to let me know the light had changed. I pulled forward. Neither of us said a word. I popped in a CD and turned up the volume.

"I'm sorry, Hudson," Alana said after about a minute. "I'm an idiot. You're right, it is pretty sad. But I'm just freaking out about seeing my mom. Forgive me?"

She reached over and put her hand on my thigh.

Not high enough to send any kind of message. Just more next to my knee. But even my knee was thrilled. Alana, it seemed, could break the unspoken rules of no-contact at will. Apparently, only I had to abide by them in Alana Land.

"Yes, I forgive you," I said, placing my right hand on top of hers. But she quickly withdrew her hand at that violation, and we reconstructed our wall.

We don't get to pick our family members. We do get to pick our friends.

>>>

The foothills were dwarfed by the Sierra Mountains, but they were still high enough to make our ears pop while we ascended. They were cold but not frosty. Warm but not balmy. They were fairy tale lands where every home looked like an old log cabin. Where tall pines pierced the sky like bayonets and icy streams carved out routes through ancient rock formations on their way to crystal blue lakes. They radiated dust—lots of it. And tangy air.

The foothills were an in-between world for people who wanted to disappear. From truth. From lies. This was where Alana Love's mother brought her daughter, Chloe, to firmly and permanently put her stamp of disapproval on Alana's father and everything he stood for. This was where she drew her battle line, as Alana put it. And it was a battle line that wasn't easy for Alana to cross.

Twenty minutes before we arrived, Alana called

her mother to let her know we'd be visiting.

"I wasn't sure if I was going to turn around at the last minute," she explained to me. "But now we're here, and you're here with me, and I know everything's going to be fine."

"What if she hadn't been here? If she was out of town or something?"

"Then we would have gone home," Alana offered simply. "No big deal."

But I knew it was a big deal for her. She was changing before my eyes, becoming smaller somehow. And frail. Is it possible a person can lose size in the face of extreme anxiety? It seemed that way. For the first time that day, I thought about Mr. Pirkle, and my mind clouded with regret. Was I failing him? Would he have another meltdown while I was away? I checked my watch to see how much time I had before Liza's nightly phone call.

>>>

The cabin was quaint and rustic. In front, a thin stream threaded its way through smooth and polished stones. The water was clear and cold. We walked single file across a narrow footbridge, and I thought I saw minnows below us, but it might have just been shadows. Wind chimes tinkled from the front porch where an empty rocker invited the weary traveler to rest underneath a sign that said *Welcome To Our Home*.

The door sprung open and out stepped a vision of Alana twenty, thirty years into the future. Her name was Heather. Heather Glen, an obviously made-up name. She took it, Alana had told me, in order to start a new life, away from the husband she claimed was emotionally abusive. Heather Glen. She was, I suppose, a hippie, if those still exist. Alana didn't believe the part about emotional abuse. In fact, she claimed it was her father who was emotionally abused by Heather. To me it seemed like everyone was throwing that term around too easily. They gave up on each other and then looked for a place to lay blame.

I could see right away where Alana's ethereal beauty came from. Heather had that same natural non-pretty prettiness. She was the falling-star, the wounded doe, the one with the obvious crack in her heart. Like mother like daughter.

So how could she walk away from her daughter, I wondered? It takes a bad parent to leave a child, no matter what Alana said. A child's natural instinct is to cling to her parent. Look for the good in them even when they're bad.

"You two can have Chloe's bed," Heather said after I was introduced. "Chloe, you can sleep with me."

Heather and Alana were carefully stepping around each other. Sizing each other up.

"We don't sleep together, Mom," Alana offered too quickly. It was strange to hear the word *Mom* directed at this stranger.

"Why not?" Heather arched her eyebrows, rippling the smooth skin on her forehead.

"We're just friends."

"Too bad," Heather laughed and Alana flushed pink. "He's a good-looking guy, this Hudson. I thought you said he was your boyfriend."

"That's Bryce."

I'm here, I wanted to say. *You're talking about a person who can hear every word you're saying.*

"Let me look at you." Heather held Alana at arm's length, hands on Alana's shoulders, feasting her eyes on the sight of her older daughter. Then she pulled her swiftly and hungrily towards her. "Give me a hug, won't you honey?"

Alana's arms hung limply at her sides, but they slowly crept up until she was clinging to her mother as if for life. Chloe watched without emotion. It was a touching but somewhat disturbing scene.

Chloe. She had none of her mother or sister's charm. Did she take after the father? I'd only seen him in passing, so I couldn't be sure. Her face was oval instead of round like Alana's. Laugh lines hadn't left their mark near the corners of her eyes or mouth. Her hair was dark and heavy. Her eyes slanted upwards and her nose was fine and straight. She was probably more traditionally beautiful than her sister and mom, but she didn't radiate like they did. She was like a black hole surrounded by brilliant stars. Soaking up energy without allowing any of it to escape.

When the hug ended, Heather turned to Chloe.

"Bring a bottle of wine and four glasses. We need

to celebrate!"

A wood stove burning in the corner of the tiny sitting room made this cabin plenty warm, but Heather brought out blankets and tucked them around us as if we were newborn babies. I accepted a glass of wine which made me glow like the corner stove. We hadn't eaten since morning, so Chloe grudgingly offered to heat up lasagna left over from their dinner. At some point, my watch alarm went off, and I stepped outside to make the call to Liza.

After a while my stomach was filled. My senses were blurred by the fire and wine and closeness to Alana, and the soft blankets wrapped so tightly I felt almost fetal. The women talked and I listened. The fly on the wall. Only there to make Alana feel safe. It wasn't about me, so I did my best to melt into the overstuffed cushions on the couch. I didn't see a TV but I saw lots of books. I recognized Alana's artwork on the wall, framed with rustic, unstained natural wood. I saw ashtrays, but no cigarettes. I think I may have nodded off for a few minutes because I had a vision of Mr. Pirkle. Demented. He'd followed me all the way there.

After a while I tuned back into the conversation and heard Heather say something about dessert, and then Chloe appeared with a plate of brownies Heather said would help us sleep.

"Don't take one," Alana hissed a warning. "They're weed brownies."

I laughed to be in on the joke, but nobody else

was laughing.

"You don't partake, Hudson?" Heather asked as though I had just come out against tooth-brushing at a dentists' convention.

"No, not for me," I said, and then quickly added so as not to appear judgmental, "it's fine, though. I have no problem with anyone else doing it."

Heather guffawed softly and, I thought, a little rudely.

Alana broke off half a brownie and picked at it for about twenty minutes. After that she got quiet and said it was time for us to go to bed.

Bed for me was a heap of cushions thrown on the floor by the side of Alana's bed. I brought along the blankets that covered us earlier. We didn't bother changing out of our clothes; we just collapsed with what we had on. No brushing teeth, no shower. Just a quick trip to the one and only bathroom to take a piss When the lights went out, Alana went out. I lay awake for a long time listening to a hooting owl just outside the window and the faint answer of its mate in the distance. The whispered breaths of sleep sliding through Alana's parted lips.

>>>

When I woke, Alana was gone. I put on some clean clothes and ran my fingers through my disheveled hair. There was no mirror in the room, but I had a good idea of what I looked like, and it wasn't a pretty sight. I grabbed my toiletry bag and made for the bathroom only to find it locked and occupied. I went back to the bedroom and blew into my cupped hands, testing for bad breath. Positive. With no other recourse, I wandered out to find the others.

I followed the sound of low voices into the kitchen. I couldn't hear the words, but I knew Alana well enough to recognize not only her voice but her mood. It wasn't happy. When I stepped into the kitchen I saw Heather and Alana sitting at the tiny table, coffee mugs in hand.

"Morning sleepy-head," Heather chirped. "Want some coffee?"

"I'll get it for you," Alana rose from her chair. "Sit. You want oatmeal? We could make pancakes, but oatmeal's easier."

"Oatmeal's fine," I said, allowing her to wait on me as compensation for my being there.

I could hear water running in the bathroom. *A shower?* I wondered how long it would be until Chloe was done. And if I could hold off, or be forced to find the nearest bush outside. It was kind of like camping, without the actual fun of camping.

After breakfast, Heather suggested a walk, so the three of us bundled up in jackets and set out along one of the deer trails that crisscrossed the vast open area surrounding the cabin. Chloe chose to stay home. From what I'd witnessed, she and Alana had exchanged less than a handful of words since our arrival and no physical signs of sisterly affection.

"Tell me about yourself," Heather said after we'd

been walking for a while.

"Hudson's an amazing artist. He's working on a graphic novel," Alana answered before I could open my mouth.

"What's a graphic novel?"

"It's laid out like a comic book, illustrated that way. But it's like a novel in terms of the length and maybe the seriousness of the topic."

"Fiction? Non-fiction?"

"It can be either. Mine will be fiction." There was no novel yet, but that much, at least, I knew would be true.

"*Will* be?"

"I haven't really started one yet. I'm still thinking through what I want to write about."

"Any ideas?" Heather asked.

"Mom, we're only eighteen. Give him a break."

"I just meant . . . is there anything compelling you want to write about?"

"Mom!"

"Yes," I answered. I didn't need Alana to run interference for me. "Lots of things."

"Like?"

"Lots of stuff," I muttered. "I just have to get it organized in my head."

I was right about that. "Stuff" was exactly what I had a lot of in my head. Lots of it.

"Do you and Alana have any classes together?"

"We're in yoga and AP Art."

"Yoga's a wonderful way to exercise the body and

mind."

"Hudson runs two businesses," Alana blurted out. I wondered why she was so intent on building me up.

"Two businesses! At your age, that's very impressive."

"At *any* age, Mom."

"At any age. Absolutely. What types of businesses, Hudson?"

I felt uncomfortable with the focus on me. I was supposed to be the fly on the wall, not the elephant in the room.

"I have a dog-walking business and another one . . ."

"Called Distress Dial," Alana interrupted, "where older people call him 24/7 for any emergency."

"How admirable. Really."

Two squirrels raced across the path just in front of us before scampering up a tree. I leaned over to retrieve a pine cone that tumbled down in their wake. I turned it around in my hand. It was flawless.

"His dad died when he was young so he and his mom have to manage on their own."

I accepted that my life had been temporarily hijacked. For whatever reason Alana displayed it like a trophy for her mother's benefit. But she was also waving it around like some kind of a sword that could cut her mother in two. She was transforming into a girl-child before my eyes, begging for her mom's approval and then attacking her when she got it. I didn't want to be anyone's model. I'd run off from responsibilities and friendships just to chase after a girl who cared nothing for the real me. The real flawed me. I hadn't even told Alana about Mr. Pirkle's private nightmare. I hadn't told her about how I'd flaked out on Fritzy's invitation to the youth retreat. The one Fritzy was so looking forward to. I tossed the pine cone into the underbrush.

"I'm sorry to hear that, Hudson," Heather said. By the lack of real emotion in her voice I knew she was wise to what was happening. "It must have been hard on you."

"His mom's great. She's really strong."

We'd arrived at a place where it was impossible to ignore the obvious. It either had to be dealt with or we all had to go off on our own separate deer trails. We'd been walking for a while so I didn't have a clue where we were or how to get back to the cabin. If I'd known, I would have left, claiming the need to use the bathroom or shower despite the disturbing thought of being alone with Chloe. Heather got right to the point.

"You know, Alana, I wanted to take both you girls with me when your father and I split up, but that wasn't possible."

"Well, I guess it might have been possible for you not to leave in the first place."

"No, that wasn't possible either."

I wondered how I should act under the circumstances. Should I pretend to admire the landscape? Pick up another pine cone? Stare at the sharp blue sky filtered through millions of pine needles? I sneezed.

"Bless you," Heather said.

"Thanks."

"Anything's *possible*. If you want to make something happen, you can. You just make that choice."

Heather sighed deeply. "Alana, my dear, I'm aware you think you know everything at the tender age of eighteen, but believe me, you don't. You'll understand when you're older."

"Oh, I will? What will I understand, Mother? How old do I have to be? Why don't you just tell me now and save me the trouble of having to figure it out on my own?"

Thankfully, the path had narrowed enough so I could drop back a few steps and get out of the line of fire.

"You'll understand that relationships don't always work out the way you hope they will. And sometimes you have to walk away for the good of everyone."

"Maybe you should have figured that out before you had kids," Alana muttered.

"What about you, Alana? Where's Bryce? Why are you here with Hudson instead of your boyfriend?"

Yeah, why are you? I thought. *Don't answer that,* I thought immediately afterwards.

"Nice try, Mom." Alana practically spat out the words. "I'm eighteen and he's my boyfriend, not my husband. I don't have kids, and besides, I'm not even going to be with Bryce after graduation. Hudson and

I are going to travel to Europe for a long time. Years maybe. Maybe forever."

"Oh, really?" Heather, suddenly noticing I was no longer next to them, turned around to look for me. "You okay with that, Hudson?"

"Umm . . . yeah. We've talked about it." I shoved my hands into my pockets.

"That's why we're here. I came to say goodbye because I won't be seeing you and Chloe for a long time. Who knows when?"

"Your father's okay with this?"

"I'm eighteen, Mom. I do what I want. Dad's always been supportive, and I'm sure I'll see a lot of him since he travels to Europe all the time."

"Oh, yes. Very supportive. Well, good for you he's so supportive. I'm sorry if you think I haven't been."

Oh, man! Why am I here? Anything would be better than this.

We all fell silent and, other than the muffled sound of footsteps on thick dust and dead, crackling pine needles, only a birdsong was audible. Once again, Heather broke the silence.

"You know why Chloe's with me and you're not? It's because she needed me more. I knew you'd be fine without me, but Chloe would never have made it with your father. She's not strong like you, Alana."

"Bullshit."

"That's not nice."

"Well, it's true. It's bullshit. You were always so busy worrying about Chloe, you never bothered about me. You think *I* didn't need a mother? You think I'm some kind of a fucking robot?"

Alana was borderline losing it.

"You're self-sufficient, Alana, in a way she's not. And your father was going to fight me for custody of one of you."

"So that was your Sophie's choice, I guess. Nice."

"You and your father always got along."

"I know. And thank God I stayed with him instead of you, or I'd be living like some kind of a freak out here in the middle of nowhere."

"Be careful what you say in anger," Heather said, without raising her voice. "Don't say anything now you might regret when I'm gone."

"When you're gone? Gone where?"

"When I'm dead. Don't harbor regrets the way I have with my own mother."

"You're *already* gone, Mother. You were never there to begin with. This is bullshit."

Alana turned around and marched right past me in the direction from which we'd just come.

"Hudson, we're leaving. Let's go home."

Heather looked at me as though somehow I was going to make everything all right. Produce a Band-Aid to patch up all those years of frustration and resentment that had rubbed them both emotionally raw. I kind of shrugged my shoulders and held out my hands. Then I turned around and trotted after Alana, the obedient puppy that I was.

"Are you sure you know the way back?" I asked

the back of her head, but she didn't acknowledge the question.

I turned around to look at Heather, but she just waved me on. She sat down on the ground and pulled her long skirt tight around her ankles. She wrapped her arms around her legs and rested her forehead on her knees. Her shoulders shuddered and I knew she was crying.

>>>

Back at the cabin, we quickly gathered our things and shoved them into our overnight bags. Chloe looked up from her book as we were just about to make an exit.

"Where's Mom?" she asked.

"She's coming later. I guess she wanted to walk some more," Alana answered, her voice somewhat softened. The lie itself was an act of compassion at least.

"Why are you leaving?"

"Hudson just remembered something he had to do back home. Something with his business. So I guess we'll see you around."

"Yeah, okay," Chloe said. She stood up awkwardly as if unsure of how to say goodbye to this alien sister of hers. She chose instead to say goodbye to me. Apparently, I was everyone's stand-in.

"Bye. Nice to meet you," she said.

"Nice to meet you too. Thanks for everything. Thanks for giving up your bedroom last night. Sorry it didn't work out that we could stay longer."

"C'mon Hudson, let's go." I knew Alana was anxious to leave before her mother got back.

"No problem." Chloe followed us out the door and watched as we climbed into the car and pulled out onto the dirt road which would eventually lead to the main road back to the highway.

Her long, thick hair, parted in the middle, hung like a curtain over her narrow white shoulders. For one brief moment, I could swear I saw all the sadness of the world contained in those slanting dark eyes from which nothing ever escaped.

"My life is a disaster," Alana finally said after we'd been driving for nearly thirty minutes.

I wasn't about to be the first one to speak. To try and summarize the catastrophe of the past two days. Disaster seemed a pretty good word for it, though.

"Don't be silly. You have brains. You have talent. Half the girls in the world would give anything to trade places with you."

"Nice try."

"I mean it." *I didn't.* "Don't talk like that. You have to look at the good things in your life. Feeling sorry for yourself isn't going to help."

Why do people always say things like that?

"Hudson. Please. I don't mean any offense, but spare me the pep talk, will you? Just be real. I know what my life is, and it sucks."

That made me mad. I wasn't exactly the happiest camper by then. I was pretty down on myself for the people I'd disappointed or pissed off the past few days. Why did *I* have to give *her* a pep talk? I could have used one myself. But I didn't say anything. I still loved her. I forgave her.

"My mom knows exactly how to insert the knife and twist. She goes for the kill every time."

"What are you talking about?"

"Well, like that whole thing of '*why are you here with Hudson and not Bryce?*' She's either clueless or cruel. And I know she's not clueless."

We had just returned to civilization, marked by the presence of asphalt roads beneath the tires. The bumpy dirt road, which had provided some distraction—at least somewhat dulled the sharp edge of emotion—was behind us. We hummed along the blacktop allowing everything to come into sharp focus. The anger and pain were tangible. They were like *things* that traveled with us, riding in the backseat of the car.

"Let me ask you a question and don't get mad at me for asking," I said.

I was feeling brave. Anger and pain egged me on from behind.

"What?"

"If we're leaving right after graduation . . . if we're going to travel to Europe and everywhere else and maybe never come back . . . why do you care what Bryce thinks? Why are you even with him anymore?"

There. I'd said it. I'd been wanting to say it ever since the day she asked me to travel with her. I looked at her out of the corner of my eye. Her mouth dropped open and then she closed it. Then it dropped open again and closed again.

"Do you love him?" I asked at last. "Are you *in love* with him?"

"I'm not *in love* with him," she shook her tousled head. "But yes, I love him."

Why did I give her the choice of loving and being in love? One and the same. A cop out.

"I guess I just don't understand that. I mean . . . what does he give you? What do you get out of the relationship? He goes off with his friends and family and doesn't invite you to come along. He doesn't offer to take you to see your mother. You don't have any of the same interests. He doesn't want the same future as you. What's the attraction?"

"The way things are between me and him, it's not what I want. If I could change him I would. But it doesn't work that way, Hudson. You don't understand because you've never been in love before."

"I thought you said you weren't *in love* with him."

"You know what I mean."

"No, I don't. I'm sorry, but I really don't know what you mean."

We were at the entrance to the highway where I could bump up my speed. Instead I pulled off to the shoulder. The car behind us honked and swerved to avoid me. As he passed us, the driver raised his middle finger just in case we didn't get the message. Anger and hurt were still there. Laughing at me.

Throwing wadded-up paper balls at the back of my head. They were making me crazy.

"What're you doing?" Alana's voice was pitched with alarm. "You can't stop on a freeway on-ramp."

"You think I've never been in love?" I dared her. "Well, I have. I'm in love with you, Alana. How have you not seen it? How could you possibly not know? You, who are supposed to be so insightful and caring."

This wasn't the way I wanted it to happen. I had visions of holding hands in the moonlight. A first kiss, where she pressed her lips to mine, greedy for my love. Staying up all night, declaring ourselves to each other. Not this. Not hurling my declaration of love at her like some kind of deadly weapon intended to inflict pain.

"Maybe I did know, okay, Hudson? I did know."

"Then why didn't you do something?" I stared furiously at the steering wheel as if *it* were the source of all my pain and anguish instead of the girl beside me.

"Because, as long as you didn't say it, it wasn't real."

I glanced in my rearview mirror. Anger and pain were gone. Hurt and desperation had taken their place.

"So now that I've said it?" I asked hopefully.

"I care for you, Hudson. Deeply."

"But you aren't in love with me?"

"I'm not in love with you."

"And you don't even love me."

"I do love you. I thought I made that clear. I care for you deeply."

Another car pulled up behind us and honked. After a few seconds, it honked again before squeezing by us on the left.

"Alana, it doesn't matter if you're in love with me or not. I can love enough for both of us. I can take care of you and make sure you'll never be unhappy again if you'll just give me a chance. Maybe you'll change when it's just the two of us and we're away from everything familiar."

"Let's not talk about this now," she said. "I'm just worried we might say something we'll regret, and it'll ruin what we do have, which is a beautiful friendship."

Her mother's daughter. But things *had* already been said that could never be taken back. Our beautiful friendship was a joke. A disaster.

Who had I become, devoid of dignity and pride? I begged for any crumb she might throw my way. But to her credit, she didn't throw crumbs or anything else. Not even an offer of gas money for the trip.

>>>

We got home after dark on Saturday, barely speaking a word to each other for hours. It was a beautiful, clear night with hot white stars punctuating the black sky. The kind of night that promised to lead to a day filled with sunshine. I dropped Alana off at her house, and we mumbled things to each other about getting together sometime soon. When

I got home Mom's car was gone, which was a good thing because I didn't feel like explaining my early and unexpected homecoming. I went in my room and dialed Fritzy's number.

"I'm back."

"How was your weekend?"

"Shitty."

"Told ya."

"Don't start. Are you still going to the retreat tomorrow?"

"Yeah."

"Am I still invited?"

"Of course."

"See you tomorrow morning then."

DO DREAMS REALLY SERVE A FUNCTION...

... or are they just a waste product? Your brain taking a dump. Because that night I eliminated a lot of crap from my brain. But it didn't exactly make me feel any better, like waking up and discovering you'd shit your pants wouldn't make you feel better even though the crap needed to come out.

In my dream, Heather was yelling at me. At *me*! And then Mom walked in and let her have it before *she* started laying into me herself. I was chasing Alana down an alley that looked a lot like the alley near her house, the one where Jennifer got his paws muddy. And then Alana disappeared, but all of a sudden there was Mr. Pirkle walking Jennifer. And I knew they were lost, but when he asked me how to get home, I couldn't explain it even though I knew the way home. It started raining and my clothes clung to me, freezing cold and dripping wet. I ran to get home before Pirkle got there. When I woke, I was breathing hard, my heart pounding, drenched in sweat as if I'd been running in real life. It was nearly dawn by then, so I laid in bed and waited for the sun to come up.

>>>

The retreat was nice since I was spending time with Fritzy. It was a church event, and I wasn't a church person, but I envied her community. The ability to focus on something bigger than yourself. To believe in a greater purpose, because I couldn't be sure everything wasn't just one crazy accident. Fritzy wasn't looking for a convert, she just wanted my company. And after two days with Alana, that was enough for me.

When I dropped Fritzy off at her house, I knew I had a boat load of homework waiting for me, but I couldn't keep my eyes off Pirkle's house. Even though I'd gotten no calls that weekend, part of me felt I'd abandoned him. And my day at the retreat was still speaking to the nobler part of myself, so I decided to check up on him.

"Want me to go with you?" Fritzy asked. "He knows me now. Even said *Hi*, to me the other day and asked how you were doing."

"Nah, I'm not staying. I'll just knock on the door and let him know I'm around if he needs anything. It's smart business to check in with your clients every once in a while. Otherwise they might wonder why they're paying you."

"Thanks for the tip, Uncle Pennybags."

"Uncle Pennybags?"

"You know…the Monopoly dude."

I didn't tell Fritzy about the dream I had where Pirkle was wandering around with Jennifer, the two of them hopelessly lost.

>>>

Pirkle was happy to see me. "Hudson!" he bellowed. "Come in. Good to see you, son."

I don't think I'd ever seen him in such a good mood.

"I was just in the neighborhood . . ."

"Of course you were. Calling on your lady." He stepped aside to let me in, closing the door behind us.

"Well, she's not really . . ." I trailed off. What was the point of denial? He was convinced Fritzy and I were having a thing (I was "sweet on her," he had once said). *Let him think what he wants.*

"She's quite a gal," he went on. "Very nice. We've spoken a few times out front."

Even though it was as far as possible from the truth, I admit to a thrill from his assumption Fritzy was my girlfriend. I'd never had a girlfriend, so no one had ever talked to me that way before. I was waiting for the wink, thump on the back, and congratulations for a job well done.

"I admire a man who's not afraid of a little height differential," he said. "You'll catch up with her one day. I can tell from the size of your hands and feet."

That was the nicest thing anyone had said to me all weekend, and I wondered if there was any truth to it. I stretched out the fingers of my right hand and did a quick, non-scientific comparison between my hand and Pirkle's.

"Did you have a nice Thanksgiving, Mr. Pirkle?"

"It was nice enough. At my age these things don't matter as much anymore. One day's the same as the next."

But I didn't think that was true. My grandparents loved Thanksgiving. And all the other holidays too.

"I went to the Senior Center," he added as if to appease me. "They did it up real nice."

"Mrs. Dickinson's been asking about you. Says she never sees you there anymore."

"I don't go often. Sometimes, when I'm in the mood. But enough about me. What brings you here today, Hudson? Am I behind on a payment?" he chuckled.

"No, nothing like that." I was going to say something about checking up on him but he seemed so . . . normal. And so grandfatherly. Who was *I* to be checking up on *him*?

"I was wondering when you might have some free time to finish our interview. The one for my government class."

"Ah, yes, the interview." He ducked his head and stared into my skull. "You sure they'd be interested in what I have to say? There are so many books written about it. People who've said it much better than I ever could."

"My teacher wants a personal perspective."

"In that case, let's go out back. We still have another hour of daylight, and it's a nice day."

I followed him out to the small cement patio. We sat in plastic molded lawn chairs, a beer bottle on the table in front of him, a glass of water for me.

"Where did we leave off?" he asked.

I scrambled to remember.

"You had a friend named Chuck who persuaded you to join the Marines. You fought in the Pacific." I glanced at the round second-story window of the neighboring house. Mr. Scolari's house.

"How old were you when you lost your father, Hudson?"

"I was ten."

"That's rough," he shook his head. "*War* is rough. It's a nasty business."

"How bad is it?" I asked. "Were you . . . were you scared?"

"Of course I was scared."

"All the time?" I thought about my father. It was a question that still haunted me.

"In the beginning, all the time. Towards the middle I was sure I was going to die, so I wasn't scared anymore. But when they told me I'd be going home, I got scared again. I had something to lose at that point, you understand."

"I think so."

"No, you don't. That was a rhetorical question."

"Oh," I said meekly.

"In Iwo Jima. That's when I knew I was a dead man. A ghost soldier. That's what protected me, I think. I had no fear so I made no false moves. When you want to live, that's when you do stupid things. Does that make sense?"

"Sort of."

"No. How could it? You'd have to be there. You'd have to experience it for yourself, otherwise it makes no sense at all."

He took a swallow of beer that must have gone down the wrong way because he went into a spasm of coughing that turned his face as pink as the sky had turned with the setting sun. When he was done, he set the bottle down and looked at me.

"Fear made me vulnerable," he said. "*Life* made me vulnerable."

"Is that a bad thing, sir?"

"You tell me, Hudson. What do you think? You're . . . seventeen years old?"

"Eighteen," I corrected him.

"Eighteen. I was two years older than you back then. Is there something you'd be willing to die for? Someone? Someone you'd be willing to fight for?"

"Yes, of course."

"You never know until you're in that situation. For me . . . I lived for the friends fighting next to me. And I lived to get back to my family. That's what I *lived* for. I died for nothing. Because I did die, you know. A part of me did die over there. For nothing."

I didn't know how you could die and live. How you could die and still continue to fight on. How you became a ghost soldier. A profound sadness came over me.

"Your friend, Chuck. What happened to him?"

"He didn't make it back. He died in my arms on that rotten little island, Iwo Jima. You've heard people say the ones who don't make it back are the heroes? Well that's the truth, Hudson. Your dad. Chuck. They're the real heroes."

I felt a lump swell in my throat.

"What was it really like? The fighting."

"You sure you want to hear all this?"

I nodded my head.

"Well, you're old enough. Old enough to fight in a war, so you're old enough to know. When people say war is hell, it's more than a cliché. It's a shabby attempt to describe something that can't be described to anyone who hasn't been through it. People ask what it's like, but they don't really want to know. It's an unspoken pact. Those of us who've been through it protect the rest of you from the reality of war. You don't want to hear about it, son. It's not all this Hollywood stuff you see in the movies. You smell the blood. The smoke. Death. That horrible stench of death you can't get out of your head. But your training takes over, and you do what you have to. Only when it's over do you stop to think about it. And if you're lucky enough, you learn to *stop* thinking about it so you can go on living."

Without meaning to, I glanced up at the round window again. Pirkle looked curiously at me for a moment before gazing at the window himself.

"What's it like to get old, Mr. Pirkle?"

"It's not too bad, Hudson. You get used to it. Slowly, over time."

"Are you scared of dying?"

He picked up the nearly empty bottle of beer and swallowed its remaining contents in two gulps.

"A little. But none of us own our time on earth. We're all just renters."

"Where's your daughter now?"

He gave me a look that told me I'd pushed too far.

"She grew up," he said quietly.

He rose from his chair and looked up at the darkening sky. He glanced at the circular window again before speaking.

"It's getting late, and I'm a little cold. You think you have enough material for your government project?" I knew he was annoyed with me for my last question. I could hear it in his voice.

"Thanks, Mr. Pirkle. I really appreciate it."

"You didn't take any notes. Think you'll remember everything?"

Stupid! Why didn't I ask for a paper and pen?

"I'm going to go home and write everything down before I forget." I picked up my empty glass and followed him inside the house.

"Thanks for stopping by," he said after showing

me to the door.

His happy mood had slipped away.

What had I just done?

>>>

When Fritzy called that night, I wasn't surprised.

"Listen, Wheeler. My dad was just outside and heard a bunch of yelling coming from Pirkle's house. He was going to call the police, but I told him not to call before talking to you."

"Tell your dad I've got it under control. I'll be right over."

"Okay," Fritzy sounded doubtful.

"Don't let him call the police. Promise me you won't."

"Okay, I got your back. You want me to go over there until you get here?"

"No, better not. I'll be there in ten."

"Ten's kind of fast."

"Let me get going. I'll be there as soon as I can."

Those days my car was on auto-pilot to the Fritzy/Pirkle zone. I parked in front of Fritzy's house because . . . well, because I didn't want to park in front of Pirkle's. As long as I was on Fritzy's side of the street, I felt the safety and strength of her nearness. Not that I was scared of Pirkle, just that he made me somewhat nervous during his evening Jekyll to Hyde transformations. Parking in front of his house made me a little less brave. A little more isolated. Funny the difference twenty or thirty feet of asphalt can make.

Fritzy was waiting outside, just like I knew she would be. She was wearing a long pink bathrobe which seemed excessively girly for her. Freed from its normal braid, her thick chocolate-colored hair flowed softly down her back, nearly to the middle. She looked amazing.

"I think he's calmed down," she said. "I haven't heard anything for the last five minutes." Her breath smelled like toothpaste.

"Might be my fault. I was asking him a bunch of questions about fighting in the war and about his daughter, too. Probably shouldn't have done that."

Our voices were soft, whispers really. I'm not sure if we were trying to be discreet or if we were just afraid of the sound of our voices discussing things we didn't understand.

"Something's gotta give, Wheeler. My dad says he can't be living there on his own if he's losing it."

"Losing it? Who told your dad he was losing it?"

Fritzy looked down at the ground and kicked the curb. She was wearing fluffy pink slippers that made her feet look twice their normal size. I leaned against my car.

"Maybe I did," she said.

"I told you stuff in confidence. And then only because you were part of the business. You weren't supposed to say anything to anyone."

"You're right, I apologize. But isn't it better he knows? The man's safety might be at stake. Why should we keep it a secret?"

The grass, black and damp with dew, glistened under the moon. A celestial reflection nestled in the corner of Fritzy's eye. Nothing in that beautiful night or that beautiful girl fit with the reality of why I was there.

"Never mind. Your dad's right. My mom says the same thing."

"So what're we going to do?"

"We . . . *I'm* going to go over there and talk him down. I think I know how to do that now. It's mainly just listening and staying calm until something inside him clicks. Anyway, thanks for calling."

"What about next time? You know it's going to happen again."

"I'm going to talk about it. I just have to be straight up with him, but not tonight. I'll do it during the day."

"Sure you don't want me to come with you?"

"No. He's used to me so it's better if I'm alone."

>>>

I put my ear to his front door but heard nothing. I knocked and then rang the doorbell. What if he'd managed to fall asleep? All the lights were on, but that wasn't unusual. I waited. Fritzy was sitting on the hood of my car, so I waved her away and motioned I was going around to the back. I wasn't so sure about using the key again, remembering the last time when Pirkle had been waiting inside with a baseball bat. I wondered if he kept a gun in the house.

I knocked on the kitchen door but he didn't come to open it. I peeked through the sliding glass door that opened onto the backyard but saw no movement in that room or the hallway beyond. Then I backed up until I could see the rearward facing bedroom window on the second floor, the only one that wasn't lit up. Sure enough, I could make out Pirkle's silhouette framed by the curtains. I waved both hands back and forth above my head but he didn't move. I imagined the binoculars pulled close to his face; the circular window facing him, the subject of his focus. I pulled out my cell phone and called his number. It rang a few times before his shadow disappeared from the window. Then a few more times until I was sure it would go to voice mail. Then silence on the other end.

"Hello?" I said to the space on the other end.

Nothing.

"Hello," I said again. It wasn't dead space. I knew he was listening. His silhouette reappeared in the window.

"Chuck?" His voice was tenuous, incredulous.

"It's Hudson, sir. I'm down here on the lawn."

"Chuck," he stated it that time like it was no longer subject to negotiation.

"I told you, sir. It's Hudson. Hudson Wheeler. I'm outside in your backyard. Can I use the emergency key to come in?"

"Hudson Wheeler. What do you know about war, Hudson Wheeler? A mollycoddled, pimple-faced kid like you?"

I have to admit I took a little offense despite the fact I knew I wasn't talking to a man in his right mind. I wasn't sure what "mollycoddled" meant, but it didn't sound good. And I'd always taken pride in my best feature, which was an acne-free complexion at the age of eighteen.

"I know nothing about war, sir. Nothing at all."

"You're damned right you don't."

I took a seat on the molded plastic chair I'd sat on earlier in the day. For the first time it occurred to me to check out the round window of Scolari's house. The light was on but no signs of life.

"Can I come in, sir?" I asked again.

"Permission denied."

That wasn't at all ambiguous. I waited for him to hang up on me but he didn't. We were two shadows conversing via radio frequency signals.

"Are you looking at the round window again?" I asked after a few minutes.

No response. He stood as straight and still as a sentry guard at the gates of a fortress.

"Mr. Pirkle, sir?"

No answer.

"Why did you think I was Chuck? He was your best friend, right?"

"A man couldn't ask for a better friend," he mumbled into the phone and for the first time I detected a slur like he'd been drinking. Maybe he had. Maybe that's what this was about.

"Could you tell me a little about him? What was he like?"

"You want to know about Chuck, Hudson Wheeler, if you really are who you say you are? I'll tell you about Chuck. I heard him call out my name that day so I crawled on my stomach and elbows to get to him. Bullets flew over my head, hitting the dirt to the right of me, to the left of me, in front of me. Everywhere but right at me. When I finally got to Chuck, he was in a bad way. *I can't move,* he said. *Put your arms around my neck, and I'll carry you on my back,* I told him. I could crawl back the way I came with him on my back. I could get him to a safe spot until a medic could treat him. But Chuck couldn't move because his legs were blown off. Both of them. He died in my arms about a minute later."

"I'm real sorry, Mr. Pirkle, sir."

"Yeah, I'll bet you are. Sorry you asked. You think your government teacher will like that story?" His voice was gravelly and choked.

"I'm sorry, sir," was all I could think of to say, and I truly was.

We resumed our silent communication and then I heard a beep. I cursed my discharging phone battery.

"What was that?" Pirkle asked.

"My battery," I said. "It's dying."

"Dying," he repeated, and I wished I'd chosen a different word.

"Mr. Pirkle," I said. "There's something I want you to know."

"What's that?"

"Fritzy . . . your neighbor. She isn't my girlfriend. She's just a friend."

"And why's that? Afraid you're not man enough to handle a big girl like her?"

"Not at all."

"Why then?"

His voice was smoothing out. The words were flowing again instead of sputtering. I thought he might be back in a world where anything was possible. Where love was possible.

"I'm in love with someone else."

"Love, hah!"

"But she doesn't love me back."

"Why not?"

"I'm not what she's looking for. What she wants."

"Then cut your losses and move on."

"How do I do that?"

"You just do it. It's part of learning how to be a man. You just do it."

"Mr. Pirkle, sir?"

"I'm still here."

My phone beeped again. It seemed like time was always running out.

"When I was a kid, my dad used to tell me if I could put salt on a bird's tail, I'd be able to catch it."

Pirkle chuckled.

"So I was always trying to get close enough to a bird to put salt on its tail, but it flew away when I got too close."

The shadow in the window shifted. I knew he was looking down at me.

"Then I tried throwing salt at them, hoping enough of it would land on their tails to keep them from flying off. But it never worked."

"You know why he said that, don't you?"

"Yeah, I finally figured it out. If I got close enough to a bird to put salt on its tail, I'd be close enough to reach out and grab it. But that could never happen because a bird would never let me get that close."

The phone beeped one final time and then nothing but dead space.

"And that's the way it is with Alana," I said to no one but myself. "Whenever I get close enough, she just flies away."

I glanced at his window but Pirkle was gone. I turned and looked at Mr. Scolari's round window. The light was off. When I got back to my car, Fritzy was nowhere to be seen, and her house was dark. I drove home and fell into a deep dreamless sleep, interrupted only by my alarm the next morning.

IS THERE A RIGHT WAY...

. . . to greet someone the first time you see her after declaring your unrequited love? Act cool in a way that borders hostility? Pretend nothing happened? Both of the above?

"Are you mad at me?" Alana asked while I unrolled my yoga mat.

I wanted to beat her to class that morning. To be positioned on my mat, looking every bit the transcendent yogi far above such earthly matters as making a fool of myself. Unfortunately, it didn't work that way.

"Why would I be mad at you?" I hated it when people said that, knowing exactly why they were mad at you.

"I mean . . . are you *upset* with me?"

"No, of course not."

Penelope still wasn't there. Neither was Gus.

"Where are the lovebirds?" I asked, lifting my chin towards the empty space by my side, normally occupied by Penelope.

"You don't know? Gus dumped her over the weekend."

"What? No, I didn't hear. I was busy on Sunday."

As if that had anything to do with why I didn't hear. I just wanted Alana to know I wasn't sitting around the house pining away for her.

"I was on the phone with Penelope most of the day. Where were *you*?"

"Fritzy invited me to a retreat that went on all day."

In the pre-declaration-of-love world, I avoided talking about Fritzy to Alana. Now it didn't seem to spark any jealous reaction that I could tell.

"So what happened with Gus and Penelope?" I asked coolly.

"Gus hooked up with some junior girl, Chelsea something."

"Hooked up?"

"Well, I don't know if they actually hooked up, but anyway, they're together, and he dumped Penelope."

No more "ha ha ha?"

"Why aren't they here?"

"Penelope called in sick, and Gus is transferring out of yoga."

"He's allowed to do that?"

"I guess. As long as he transfers into a comparable class—any other zero period PE."

I knew I should have said something like "Poor Penelope. Gus is such a dick." Those kinds of sympathetic statements would have gotten me on Alana's good side. But all I could think was: *Gus Ligety, already on his second relationship before Christmas break, and I still haven't even kissed a girl. Life is unfair.*

"Wow," I mumbled.

"Anyway, I'm sorry about this past weekend," she whispered as Ms. Senger took attendance.

I pretended not to hear. Hearing would require a response. A response would require diving into a whole lot of things I didn't want to talk about anymore.

>>>

"Here," Alana shoved a wad of bills into my hand. "I hope it's enough to pay for gas."

It was passing period, and the money was unexpected. I didn't care so much about the cash, although I always needed it. What I did care about was what I perceived to be Alana's self-centeredness. But if I was wrong about the gas money, maybe I was wrong about that too.

"Hudson, could you pick me up after school today?"

I thought about the talk I was supposed to have with Pirkle. I could do it early.

"Where's Bryce?"

"I don't want to be dependent on him for rides home anymore."

"O-kay. Yeah, I guess so. You coming over afterwards?"

"Yes!" she pressed her hands together under her chin and smiled angelically. "Promise you'll wait for me to walk the dogs. We can do it together."

"Okay, sounds good."

"I miss Jennifer. I miss them all!"

"I'm sure they miss you too," I answered, perhaps not so convincingly. She'd only walked the dogs with me a few times.

"And Hudson, let's work on our graphic novels together. Maybe we can get some dinner too."

"Your dad's not around?"

"He's traveling this week," she said.

"Maybe. Let me see how much work I get done before you come over. I'm way behind."

It was true but I was also still playing it cool. And it was a fact I hadn't overcome my writer's block—there wasn't any graphic novel to work on. I could've just been honest, but art was where I stood out for Alana. Head and shoulders above the masses. A possible equivalent to the starting quarterback.

Then, on my way to Pirkle's I got a text from Alana: *I don't need a ride home anymore. Thanks anyway. Oh, and sorry, but I won't be able to walk the dogs with you, I'm spending the night at Cherie's and having dinner there too. See you tomorrow. Love ya! xoxo*

Cherie was in our art class, and lately she'd been spending a lot of time at our table, looking over our shoulders and visiting with Alana. What can I say?

Not only was I jealous of Bryce, now I was jealous of Cherie too. And disgusted at myself.

Cut your losses and move on, Pirkle had said. *Part of learning how to be a man.*

How did this magical thing happen where you become a man and learn how to control your feelings instead of letting them control you? When would it happen for me?

I rang Pirkle's doorbell, hoping to catch him at home while at the same time hoping I wouldn't. The talk was a monumental task but avoiding it was worse. I was already dreading my nights, worried when I'd be called to handle the next meltdown. Maybe there'd come a night I wouldn't be able to talk him down—then what? I didn't want it to be just *my* problem anymore.

"Hudson," he said, when he opened the door. "Twice in two days?"

"Could we talk?"

>>>

Once again on his back patio. Once again, sitting on the molded plastic chair. My mouth was so dry it felt like I was coughing up my words.

"What brings you here?" Pirkle asked. "I'm not sure the piddling amount I pay you justifies all these visits."

I made a mental note of "piddling." I thought my rates were high, but if he considered them *piddling* I should probably consider raising them. If I divided my monthly rate by the amount of hours I'd spent at Pirkle's, I'd have been way better off sticking with dogs.

"I'm not sure how to say this . . ." I began and then stopped. I couldn't bring myself to make eye contact. I froze. Stage fright of sorts.

"Just say it, son. What's the problem? You shutting down the business?"

"No, nothing like that. I want to talk to you about what's been going on at night."

"At night?"

He was genuinely puzzled; I could see it in his eyes. He looked above my head towards the round window of Scolari's house. It took all my self-control to resist turning around and doing the same thing myself. The window had become a candle light, and we were the moths, unable to resist its allure. I knew why he looked, but why did I?

"Maybe you know what's going on, but maybe you don't," I mumbled. "It began a while ago when I started getting phone calls from you at night. And I couldn't make any sense out of what you were saying. Then there've been the times when I've come over at night. You weren't exactly yourself." A feeling of shame washed over me as though I had no right to accuse this imposing man of such lapses.

He looked down at his hands which were folded on the table. I looked at them too. Spotted with age, threaded with ropey veins, disfigured by swollen joints, his hands looked ancient. It was a wonder those same hands once held a weapon that helped win a war. That had been bathed in blood while cradling a dying friend. That had held a woman at a USO dance, twirling her around the dance floor while she fell in love. That had held the hand of a little girl with ringlets in her hair. It seemed impossible.

"Do you remember the burglary?" I asked. He should at least remember it since the two of us had cleaned up the mess during broad daylight. "I've been thinking about what happened. I mean, there wasn't any sign of forced entry, and you didn't want to call the police."

He didn't say anything.

"If you don't remember all those times I came over at night, I could fill you in on what happened."

Had I gone too far?

Finally he spoke. "You're right, Hudson. It's been too much. This isn't what you bargained for, nor should you have to deal with it. I'm canceling my subscription effective immediately."

A wave of relief washed over me. This was what I really wanted, wasn't it? If I was completely honest with myself. To be free of Mr. Pirkle and the living nightmare that came from our association. But then I felt sick with shame. What was I thinking? That I'd stand up, offer my hand and say, *Thank you very much, it's been a pleasure doing business with you.* And then walk out of his life and leave him to . . . leave him to what? I didn't even know.

"No. Mr. Pirkle, sir. Please. That's not why I came

here today. I don't want to lose you as a client. I just want to . . . *help* if I can."

He looked up at the window again and then down at his carefully folded hands.

"Tell me what you've seen, Hudson. When you've come over at night. Don't hold anything back for my sake."

So, I told him everything. The baseball bat. The underwear. The combat boots. The harsh, out-of-character words. The yelling the neighbors heard. The phone calls. The circular window where he swore he saw his daughter.

"I'm losing my marbles, aren't I?" he said when I was done. He sounded resigned, rather than sad. "Sometimes I wake up in the middle of the night and I smell it. I feel it. And there I am again."

"Do you remember any of it? Any of the stuff I just said?"

"Some of what you've said sounds familiar. Some of it doesn't."

"I've done some research online, Mr. Pirkle. And my mother's a nurse so she's told me a few things."

"Your mother?" he said sadly. "She knows about this too?"

"Yes, sir."

I hoped he wouldn't ask if I'd told Fritzy, and luckily, he didn't. But I'd told him the neighbors heard yelling. Maybe he didn't have to ask, he already knew.

"I'm ashamed of myself, Hudson," he said. "That it's come to this."

"Don't be ashamed, sir. Maybe it's just a vitamin deficiency. Maybe there's some medication that could help. My mom says you should see a doctor."

"I'm not going to see a doctor," he brought his closed palm down forcefully on the glass table, rattling our drinks and my nerves. "They'll lock me up in the loony bin. I'd just as soon die then go into some . . . facility."

"What if they can cure you?"

"Cure me? There's no cure for old age, Hudson. And anyway, how do you think I got to be ninety years old? By running to the doctor every time I had a bloody nose? No, it was because I stayed away from doctors for the past fifty years. They *have* to find something wrong with you, or they go out of business. And if they can't find something, they invent something."

The obvious response was the hardest thing I'd ever had to say.

"But there *is* something wrong with you, Mr. Pirkle . . . sir."

My goal was to get the name of someone who would help me convince Pirkle to see a doctor. But he didn't seem to have anyone in his life outside of Mrs. Dickinson and other casual acquaintances from the Senior Center. You'd think if you live for ninety years you'd have children, grandchildren, nieces, nephews, neighbors, *somebody*. But if you have no children, no wife. If you're an only child like me. Then what? What if you don't go out anymore to socialize? What if there's no network of friends?

His daughter was my only hope. I knew she existed. I'd seen her picture, and he'd told me she was grown up, so that meant she might still be alive.

Then where was she?

"When I came back from the war, I wasn't much good for anything, but there was a gal waiting at home for me, so we got married."

"Why?"

"What else do you do? You grow up. You get a job. You get married."

Ugh. Depressing thought. That's all there is?

"Then of course the children start coming. Back in those days, people didn't sit around and plan families. We did what nature intended us to do."

Was it really that bad? No joy in any of it?

"You have to understand, I was numb when I came home. My feelings seemed to go through a strainer that filtered out all the good stuff other people felt. What came out the other end didn't amount to much."

What about his wife? Did she know he was suffering?

"My wife knew something was wrong. She cried for me every night. *She* cried, but I couldn't even cry for myself. I couldn't make her feel better, and I couldn't make myself feel better either."

And how did it end?

"I tried to find the humanity in my enemy in order to move on. But when I couldn't find it in the enemy, I started to doubt it in myself. And once I knew there was no humanity in me, I ceased to be of any use to my family. After that, it was easy to cut them loose . . . my wife and daughter. They needed to get on with their lives, and they weren't going to do that with me hanging around. I sent money and made calls from time to time, but when my wife remarried she didn't want anything from me anymore. She broke off all contact, and I'm ashamed to say I was relieved."

And there was never another chance at love?

"Don't get me wrong, I kept the company of women after my divorce. I wasn't dead below the waist, if you get my meaning. I was just dead above it."

His daughter? No reconciliation?

"Maybe my daughter knew about me, and maybe she didn't. But another man raised her. Provided for her and loved her. Bandaged up her scraped knees and eventually gave her away in marriage. Who was I to get in his way?"

So I was alone. If someone was going to get help for Mr. Pirkle, it was going to be me. But I had support. I had friends. I had Mom and my aunt, uncle, cousins, and grandparents. Even Mrs. Dickinson would help if I asked her, which of course I couldn't because of privacy issues. But in the end it would be up to me, and I knew I wouldn't abandon him.

"You know, Hudson. The last time I saw my daughter's pretty little face was the day I drove away from the house after my wife and I had our final words. Something made me stop and turn around to take a last look. There was a round window in the front of our house and Maggie would stand up on a little wooden box and peer through the window when it was getting close to time for me to come home from work. Then the minute she saw my car turning onto that country lane, stirring up a cloud of dust behind me, she'd run outside and wait 'til I drove up and got out. That day . . . the day I left . . . I turned around, and there she was. Looking right through the window. That was the last time I saw her."

"Maybe that's why you think you see the face of your daughter at night. The round window, just like the one in your old house. You once told me you thought you were in your old house. It's probably a repressed memory or something."

"Or it's just a girl who lives in that house, more likely," Pirkle chuckled, and I was slightly annoyed he brushed me off like that.

"There isn't a girl who lives in that house. I know the guy who lives there, and he's a piano teacher named Mr. Scolari. He's single and doesn't have any kids. He lives alone like you." I tried to deliver this news calmly, keeping any emotion out of my voice. I knew I wasn't succeeding. I wondered why, Pirkle and Scolari being the backyard neighbors they were, had never met or conversed.

Pirkle glanced up at the window behind me. He'd been looking there frequently during our conversation but I was determined not to turn around. I didn't want to feed into his fantasy or hallucination or whatever it was.

"Hudson," he said without shifting his gaze from the window. "She was there the whole time you were talking. You missed her."

I felt a flash of anger. Wasn't I the one putting myself out there for him? And if I was, didn't he owe me some respect? He could at least pretend to play along. Maybe I should have told him how close the neighbors came to calling the cops. How close he was to being escorted to the nearest mental health facility in the middle of the night. And why me? I was just the guy who'd come up with an easy way to make a few extra bucks. I hadn't signed up for this.

"I have an idea," I said as calmly as I could. "Come with me to Mr. Scolari's house. Take a look around. See for yourself there's no girl in the window."

"And say what? *Good afternoon, Mr. Scolari. Mind if I take my batty old friend on a tour of your home? He's been spying on you and wants to see your little girl.* No thank you, Hudson. Appreciate it if none of this goes any farther. I know your mother's involved now, but let's keep it at that. Next thing you know I'll be arrested as a peeping Tom, or worse."

"What if I go over there alone, and I won't tell him why I'm there. I'll make an excuse to go upstairs, and I'll call you while I'm looking out the window. Would you believe me then?"

"I think I'd believe just about anything you told

me, son, unless I thought you didn't know any better. I know you're a man of your word."

"If I do that. And if I can prove to you there's no girl in the window . . . would you agree to see a doctor?"

"I'd give it careful consideration. I suppose I'd have to, if that was the case."

>>>

By the time I left Pirkle's house, Fritzy was already home from school. An older model orange BMW was pulling out of her driveway. Behind the wheel, a tall, blond guy. His massive square head nearly touched the interior ceiling. His shoulder was so broad it half stuck out of the open window. I stood on Pirkle's side of the street until he drove off.

"What're you waiting for?" Fritzy called from across the street. "Come on over!"

"Who was *that*?" I inclined my head towards the vanishing Beemer.

"Friend of mine."

Was it my imagination, or were her cheeks glowing? Were her eyes sparkling?

"He looks kind of . . ."

"Kind of what? Jockish? Like me? Say it, Wheeler."

"Nothing. Have you ever mentioned him before?"

"Probably not. You never ask about my personal life. We're always too busy talking about yours."

A car pulled into the driveway. Fritzy's mom with the giant child in tow.

"Hi, Frankie. Hi, Mrs. Fritz."

"Hello, Hudson," her mother sung out. An expensive looking messenger bag was slung across her shoulder. She wore a long-sleeved cobalt-blue blouse and a tight gray wool skirt. Her black heels added an extra three or four inches to her already awesome height. Her hair was cut straight across and barely brushed her shoulders. It was strong, shiny hair like her daughter's. Fritzy looked like her mom but had her dad's direct personality. And jawline.

Frankie leaned over to retrieve his backpack and grimaced at me, although I knew it was just his version of a smile. He didn't talk a lot. He headed straight for the door and after a few more words and a peck on her daughter's cheek, Mrs. Fritz followed him in.

"How was school today?" I asked.

I picked up the basketball and passed it to Fritzy. Ball play was almost becoming second nature to me.

"As good as can be expected." She took a shot and swished it. "Why are you here?" She passed the ball back to me.

"I had the talk with Pirkle."

I dribbled standing in place, first one hand three times, then the other hand three times. She tapped it away from me and took another shot. Made it again.

"And?"

"And it went better than I thought. But worse than I hoped." I got the rebound and dribbled again. Three with one hand. Three with the other. A form of ball meditation.

"What does that mean exactly? Can you do something with the ball please? Take a shot."

"It means I need to ask you for a favor."

I took my shot and banked it in. I sat down on the driveway and held the ball between my ankles.

"Could we go over to Scolari's house sometime soon?" I asked. "You'd have to come with me. And maybe keep him busy while I run upstairs and call Pirkle."

"The girl in the window?"

Fritzy loved a good mystery, and I could tell she was hooked. She sat down next to me.

"Yup. I have a deal with him . . . or at least I hope I do. If I can prove there's no girl in the window, he'll go see a doctor and tell them what's been going on."

"He actually said that, or that's what you're hoping?"

"He said he'd think about it, which is a big step forward."

"Why don't we just tell Scolari the truth?"

"Pirkle would have my ass. He'd be upset if he even knew I'd told *you* everything."

"Does he think I'm deaf and can't hear what goes on at night?"

"We can't tell Scolari, okay? No matter whether you think it's right or wrong, that's just the way it has to be."

"Why's it so important? That girl in the window stuff?"

"Because he thinks he's normal . . . old age changes he can handle on his own. But the girl in the window, that's like seeing something that isn't really there. Crazy time. Today he saw her in the middle of the day. Usually it happens at night so I think he's getting worse."

"I don't see why it'd be a problem to go to Scolari's house. All we have to do is think of a reason to be there. When do you wanna go?"

"The sooner the better. Today. Right now."

"My brother has a lesson in an hour. Scolari might be home now. Let's go see."

>>>

In the time it took us to walk to Scolari's house I came up with five different excuses for knocking on his door, four of which Fritzy rejected. The surviving excuse was a bad one, but it would have to do.

"Let's rehearse it one more time," I said. "We knock on the door. You do the talking. You tell him we were just taking a walk and wondered if he had a beginner's piano book I could borrow. Then I ask if I could use the bathroom and you ask for a glass of water while I run upstairs and call Pirkle from the window. Got it?"

"This is so lame, Wheeler. He's going to think we're crazy."

"Just please talk to him like you really mean it. If you come off like we're telling the truth, then he'll believe it. I promise I won't ask you to do anything like this again."

"It's kind of like this show I saw once where . . ."

"Will you do it?"

She picked up a pebble and threw it across the driveway.

"Okay, but only because we're business partners."

"Friends," I corrected her.

"Wheeler?"

"What?"

"You've got some daredevil in you. Who would've thought?"

>>>

"Lauren." Scolari seemed surprised and slightly flustered at the sight of us on his doorstep.

I could never get used to the idea that Fritzy possessed an actual real girl's name.

"Hi, Mr. Scolari," she blurted out in a most unconvincing monotone. "We just came by to get a book for Wheeler."

He stepped onto the front doorstep, allowing the door to swing shut behind him.

"What kind of book?"

"I was wondering if I could borrow a beginner's piano book," I picked up the slack. Acting wasn't my specialty but anything was better than Fritzy's pathetic attempt. "To kind of study for a few weeks."

"Have you gotten a piano since we last talked, Hudson?"

"No, but I'm seriously considering it." I couldn't

imagine myself sitting side by side with this guy for the hundreds of hours it would probably take me to learn even the simplest of tunes.

"Could I have a glass of water?" Fritzy sputtered.

"We've been walking," I said. "It's pretty hot today."

"For December, I suppose." The tips of his eyebrows seemed to reach for each other just above his nose.

"And Wheeler—I mean Hudson—was wondering if he could use your bathroom."

I was ready to kill her for her appalling lack of acting skills and timing. But Fritzy was an open book which was part of her charm. What you saw was exactly what you got, and would I have liked her as much if she'd been a talented liar?

"No, I'm fine. I don't have to go." My face flushed hot with embarrassment. Something about him made me not want to share any information about my bodily functions. He was so neat. So self-contained. So distant. I didn't believe he would ever use someone else's bathroom or want someone to use his.

"But I really *am* thirsty," Fritzy said.

"I tell you what. I'm pretty busy, kids. I have a few things I need to take care of before heading over to your house, Lauren. I'll bring some books along for Hudson and leave them with you."

He completely ignored the part about Fritzy being thirsty.

"Okay, we'll see you, Mr. Scolari," she said.

"Thanks for letting us stop by," she added.

Our first attempt at detective work was a disaster, in spite of all the crime shows Fritzy watched. That should have been a warning we paid attention to.

"Okay, that just happened," I said once we were safely out of earshot.

"Or didn't. What the hell, Wheeler? *No, I don't really have to go to the bathroom.*" Her high-pitched imitation of my voice was depressing.

"I hope you're not planning to audition for the school play. Come on! A little inflection in your voice goes a long way. I mean . . . you did a better job of imitating me just now then you did acting like yourself. Who *were* you back there?"

"Oh, shut it," she snapped back. "Now what are we going to do?"

"I'm going to have to think of something else. I can't go back and tell Pirkle, *oh by the way, the guy who lives in the house wouldn't let us in.* Then he'd really be suspicious."

"It would totally fuel his paranoia. That's what he has, right?"

"What do you mean, that's what he has?"

"He has paranoia, right?"

"No, dementia."

"Oh well, same thing."

"No, it's not."

"Enough with your nitpicking, Wheeler. Get busy and think of plan B. And when you do, let me know what my part is."

It was discouraging. I was so anxious to pull it off and get the whole mess behind me, I'd rushed into it without thinking it through. It wasn't Fritzy's fault we failed, it was mine.

"I'm sorry I got mad at you," I said. "It was a bad plan, but I'll think of something else. The important thing is to get Pirkle to a doctor."

"You're right about that."

"But Fritzy? Was it just me or do you think he acted kind of weird? I mean, why wouldn't he let us in. Frankie's his star pupil."

Fritzy appeared to ponder this for a few seconds. "My guess," she said. "He was entertaining. You know." She jabbed me in the ribs with her elbow.

"Ouch!" I pushed back. "No, I don't know. I'm just saying, he strikes me as odd, that's all."

"You have a feeling?" Her eyes lit up.

"Maybe . . . I can't put my finger on it exactly."

"Or are you just getting paranoid like Pirkle. You'd better be sure when you say something like that, Wheeler. Some people might say you were a little odd yourself."

"Well, you're definitely odd," I said. Another elbow jab.

We'd walked back to Fritzy's by then. My car was parked across the street at the curb in front of Pirkle's house. I automatically looked at his kitchen window to see if he was watching but he wasn't there. I eyed the distance between where I was standing and my car to calculate the number of seconds it would take me to reach it at a full run, climb in, and shut the door behind me.

"Oh, and Fritzy?"

"Yeah?"

"Your boyfriend looks like an orangutan."

She got me square in between the shoulder blades with the basketball before I ever made it to the car.

>>>

Plan B. What should that look like? Here's what I did know:

1. Pirkle was getting worse

2. Either my mom or Fritzy's dad would step in if I didn't take care of it

3. Pirkle was still a man who deserved to live life on his own terms.

At home, Buster was waiting for me on the other side of the sliding door which opened onto my backyard. Since the glass was smeared with his nose prints, he'd possibly been there the whole day. He stood up on hind legs, scratching wildly at the glass that separated us, his one good eye sparkling with joy at the sight of me.

"What the hell, Buster?" I opened the door and he darted inside, looking around for the nearest chew object with which to relieve his frustration.

I checked the loose board separating his yard from mine to discover he'd finally figured out how to manipulate it on his own.

Back inside, he was chewing on one of my shoes.

"Okay, Buster. Let's get the gang, and you can take your walk."

He looked up at me sullenly when I ripped the shoe from his mouth.

The doorbell rang.

"Hey," Bryce said just as casually as if we were finishing up a conversation begun only minutes earlier. "Alana here?"

Buster squeezed through my ankles to get a better look at this ringer-of-doorbells.

"Nope."

I knew where Alana was. Knew she'd gone home with Cherie and was staying over that night. But was it my job to make Bryce's life easier by keeping tabs on his girlfriend? I didn't think so.

"Funny dog," he chuckled, looking down on Buster. "What happened to his eye?"

"He banged his head on a table, and it popped out," I said.

With his one eye fixated on Bryce, Buster wagged his scrawny tail furiously, irrationally disappointing me. Bryce leaned over to scratch him behind the ear.

"Poor little guy," he said. "Mind if I come in for a glass of water?"

I'd used the glass of water ploy only an hour earlier with Mr. Scolari, so I wasn't completely falling for it.

"Sure."

He followed me into the kitchen where I handed

him a bottled water and waited for him to leave. But he was in no hurry. He emptied the contents in about four or five big gulps, all the while looking around.

"So, this is where you live," he remarked when he was done, just as though something historical had once happened in that kitchen.

"Yup. This is where I live."

Why wasn't he leaving?

He stared at the note on the refrigerator, pronouncing a sort of *hmph* after a few minutes, then turned his attention to the family room (which you could see from the kitchen) where the TV and video games where hooked up.

"Wanna play?" he motioned to the video game controllers.

"I can't right now," I said. "Gotta take the dogs for a walk before their owners get home."

"Oh, right. The dogs."

He walked into the family room. Buster and I followed him there. He looked out into the yard through the sliding glass door.

"How's art?" he asked without turning.

"Fine."

"Alana says you're really talented. She's always talking about that."

He strolled back to the kitchen with Buster and me still trailing behind him.

"She's exaggerating," I said to his back. "I'm not that good."

"No really, you are. I've seen some of the stuff

you've done. Alana's got a few of your pieces hanging on her bedroom wall."

Insert knife and turn. I still hadn't seen the inside of Alana's bedroom.

"Well, thanks."

What was that expression about waiting for the other shoe to drop? Because it sure as hell felt like something had already dropped.

"Think I could have another bottle of water to take with me? I'm not going home for a while."

"No problem," I said and handed him another one.

Go. Leave. Get out. I didn't want to feel guilty about being in love with his girlfriend and I didn't want to establish any human connection with him either.

"You're not lying to me are you?" The smirk on his face was both arrogant and anxious. It surprised me I might actually be able to provoke some anxiety in this alpha male.

"Lying?" Were we still having a friendly talk or had we just completed a conversational U-turn? "About what?"

"Is Alana really here?" he asked.

"Of course not." I was dumbfounded. "Why would I lie about that?"

Here was my second chance to tell him where Alana was, but I stubbornly refused.

"Mind if I take a look around?"

"You're being ridiculous," I said. But I couldn't

resist the idea of watching Bryce act like an idiot. "Go ahead if you want."

He stared at me for what seemed like a minute, as though allowing his truth-o-meter to get an accurate reading. Then he dropped his eyes to Buster who was busily adoring him. He looked back at me.

"Are you trying to steal Alana from me?" he asked. "Don't bother, because you can't, and you might make a fool out of yourself in the process."

He was right about that.

"Look, why don't you just go and find Alana because she's not here. I'm not trying to steal her away from you, and by the way you can't steal people. They do whatever they want."

There was the anxious and arrogant smirk again.

"I'll see you around," he said. "Thanks for the water."

He bent over to scratch Buster behind the ear and then headed out the door.

> > >

I couldn't stop thinking about Bryce's visit but didn't mention it to Alana the next day. The thought of the two of us fighting over her like dogs wasn't an image I wanted implanted in her brain.

"I heard Bryce came to your house looking for me yesterday," she whispered in between yoga poses.

Penelope turned her head in our direction so as not to miss a word. With Gus gone, Penelope paid a lot of attention to me, as if I had the power to deliver Gus back to her. The thought occurred to me she might even want to use me for some revenge sex which I wasn't totally opposed to. I did feel sorry for her. Even her *ha ha's* lacked real enthusiasm. Nothing was *"the cutest thing ever"* anymore, and she no longer cared if you could *"believe it."* And I actually missed Gus. I'd become the last guy standing. In yoga, at least.

"Yeah," I wondered how much she knew. "Did he ever find you?"

"We got together last night."

"Oh, I thought you were staying with Cherie." I prickled with irritation.

"I was but . . ." she trailed off. "Anyway, thanks for not saying where I was because I might *not* have wanted to see him."

Did she think this was all one big conspiracy? Me and her scheming together to manipulate Bryce into loving her the way she wanted to be loved?

"You're welcome, I guess."

"I don't need a ride home today," she said.

"I didn't offer one."

I was right on the cusp of where love turns to hate.

>>>

Fritzy called after school.

"So, what's plan B?"

"I haven't figured it out yet."

"Well, you'd better. Pirkle was out in his front yard

last night in just his tighty-whities and boots. He was carrying a shovel over his shoulder."

I got a sick feeling in the pit of my stomach.

"Why didn't you call me?"

"I was going to, but he went inside. I didn't want to bother you unless I had to."

"Shit."

"When are you going to come over and get your piano books? Scolari left a stack of them for you."

The piano books. My failed plan A. The sick feeling turned into a cold, hard lump.

"I guess I can come a little later."

"Wear your workout clothes. We can shoot some hoops."

>>>

I walked into Fritzy's house and dumped my keys in the brass metal bowl kept on the entry table just for that purpose.

"One sec while I get my shoes on," she said. I followed her into the bedroom.

Every square inch of wall space in her bedroom was taken up by posters of glistening bodies of athletes in motion; musculature displayed to prime advantage.

"Jesus, Fritzy. Your bedroom's like a muscle shrine."

"You're getting there." She slipped a shoe on and drew the laces tight. "Slowly but surely."

"So anyway . . ." I sat on the thick, spongy carpet,

my back to the wall.

"What?"

"I'm not sure I'm allowed to talk about myself anymore since you said that's all we do."

"Go ahead, Wheeler," she sighed. "What's going on with Love now?"

"Yesterday Bryce came over looking for her. He thought she was at my house hiding from him."

Fritzy stopped mid-shoe and looked up at me with disbelief.

"No way!"

"And he wanted to look around my house to make sure she wasn't there. I told him to go for it, but he must have realized how stupid that was, so he left. But not before telling me I'd better not try to steal her away from him."

Fritzy pulled on her other shoe and yanked the laces upward before tying and double tying them.

"That's what you're trying to do, isn't it? Steal her away from him."

"No. I mean . . . of course I'd love it if she left him, but it's so demeaning to say that. Like she's a piece of property he owns, and I can somehow . . . take her away from him."

"You would if you could."

She sat forward on the edge of her bed and directed the Fritzy glare right at me. I consciously prevented myself from sliding any further down the wall.

"Anyway," she stood up as our signal to leave, "I

don't know what you see in that girl, but you should have fought him even if you got your ass handed to you."

I stood up too.

"Fought him? Alana abhors violence. She even thinks sports are too violent."

"What the hell does 'abhor' mean?"

"She hates it."

"Oh. Well you should have at least punched him."

With her hands on her hips she looked like a warrior princess preparing for battle.

"Fritzy, you have many fine qualities, but common sense isn't always among them."

"Look who's talking, Mr. Smarty Pants."

"Anyway, you don't even know Alana."

"Thank God for that," she said. "C'mon let's go."

THE CANADIAN GEESE WERE GETTING FAT...

. . . or at least their bird shit was. Canadian geese fly south to winter in my town and others like it. Because I lived only a few blocks from a tiny lake, I'd usually find one or two in my front yard that time of year. I had to admit they were beautiful, elegant with that white band under their chin like they were wearing tuxedos. But they were also mean and nasty, whipping their long necks at me, hissing whenever I walked to my own front door, forced to step around their slimy shit. One day, a few of them landed in Buster's backyard, and I had to vault over the fence to save him from a massacre.

With Christmas break just a week away, Alana gave Bryce an ultimatum. "Hawaii or me," she said.

"It's not that I don't want him to have his own friends and do his own thing. It's just that other guys invited their girlfriends to go with them and he didn't. So what does that tell you?"

She looked to me for the answer, but what she really wanted was confirmation. He was a jerk, callous and selfish. But the messenger often gets killed, don't they? What I wanted was for her to come to that conclusion on her own. And eventually she did.

"I'm over him, Hudson," she said one night on the phone. "He made his choice, so I made mine."

Her decision turned her into an even unhappier girl. Penelope and Alana were so bonded in their misery I thought I felt actual gamma rays of grief passing between them (through me) during yoga class. They were sisters in sorrow, with Cherie always willing to jump in and wallow with them even though (so far) she hadn't yet been victimized by a heartless guy. I became the enemy sex.

"Get over it," I advised her. "If it's not working for you, then move on."

Wasn't this what Pirkle had advised me to do? Yes. *Did I do it?* No.

"I thought he was like us, Hudson, but I guess I was wrong. He got sucked into that whole football thing and couldn't handle it."

"I'm not sure I get what you mean."

"I mean that even if he wanted me to go to Hawaii with him, I'm not the typical high school jock girlfriend. I don't fit the mold. And he wasn't strong enough to stand up to the pressure of the other guys on the team."

"He seems like he's pretty good at standing up to

pressure. Being the quarterback of the team is a lot of pressure." The devil in me went for the kill. "Maybe he just didn't want you to come, have you ever thought of that?"

She got real quiet after that, and I was pretty sure she was mad at me—killing the messenger and all—but the next night she called to talk again. We'd been doing a lot of our visiting by phone those days, with Penelope and Cherie monopolizing her after-school time.

"I've been thinking about what you said, and I think you're right. I think Bryce is just not that into me. Maybe I was fun and exciting to begin with when he was ostracized from his group and could have sex with me anytime he wanted."

Sex? Anytime he wanted? With Alana?

I always knew that was a possibility, but I tried not to think about it, and we never discussed it until that moment. Of course, a guy like Bryce wouldn't stay with a girl who wasn't putting out. He wasn't desperate like me. My throat got tight with the idea of sex on demand from Alana Love. Too tight to deliver an appropriate response.

"Hudson? You there?"

"Yeah."

"Anyway. I just wanted to tell you something really exciting. My dad's taking me to Paris for Christmas. It's gonna be amazing. I'll check everything out for when you and I go."

"Cool," I said.

Christmas lost some of its luster with Alana so far away in Paris. She texted me pictures of the places we'd visit when we went back there together, but they didn't do anything for me. For her they were experiences, soon to be great memories. For me they were just tiny images on a phone screen. I could go online and find better pictures than those.

Fritzy and I made a pledge to run together every day of vacation. Whenever I ran with her, I knew she held back for my sake. Even if I could match her strength and endurance, which I couldn't, I could never match the length of her legs. One of her strides equaled about one-and-a-half of mine. But I knew I made up for what I lacked by keeping her company. And she did get a certain satisfaction in witnessing my physical transformation.

One day she was unusually quiet during our run, and when we were done, she suggested going out to grab a burger. I waited for her to shower and change, and then we went over to my place where I did the same. After dinner, we drove around in her truck throwing out scenario after scenario for plan B, all the while wasting a whole lot of gas. We finally parked on top of Windy Hill, which was a well-known make-out spot late at night. But being so early in the evening (and on a weeknight) we had the place to ourselves with its more innocent reputation as just a park.

Below us the city twinkled to life. Above us, the night sky did the same. Windy Hill lived up to its name that night, whipping up a chill that somehow pierced even the steel doors of the truck. Fritzy turned the key in the ignition and left the heater running. Alana was on my mind. Plan B was on my mind. Homework was on my mind. Homework, in fact, was always on my mind those days when school structure was something I actually missed. Life as a home-schooled student meant never being done. Some project. Some test. Some reading was always lurking somewhere in the back of my mind.

"Wheeler," she said, shaking me from my thoughts, "I'm sorry, I know I've been hard on you."

"About what?"

"About Love. I guess you can't help it if you're hung up on her. It's just that sometimes I get frustrated with you, and I don't get it."

"That's okay. Sometimes I don't get it either."

"Are you still going to Europe with her after graduation?"

"That's the plan. Why?"

"I don't know. It just makes me sad to think of it."

"You'll be off at college. We wouldn't be seeing each other anyway."

"Maybe not, but I think we would. We'd find a way to make it happen."

I didn't ask her *how* that would happen. Fritzy wasn't a great student, but she was a great athlete, and she was going to a great college, one I'd never have a chance of getting into. And anyway, the two colleges my mom made me apply to were in-state. Fritzy would be all the way across the country.

But I was sharing in her blues that night. Maybe it was the remoteness of the hilltop. Maybe it was the reminder of the season, the passage of time, my mounting disappointments, Alana so far away. Maybe I *was* thinking of Fritzy and the idea that after graduation our worlds would be so different—her with her fancy athletic scholarship, me traveling the world. So different that one day we might even forget what it was that had once brought us together.

"Have you ever kissed a girl, Wheeler?"

That rocketed me right out of my gloom. I always lie more convincingly when there's a kernel of truth buried somewhere in the lie so I thought about the kiss my mom routinely planted on my cheek whenever she said goodnight.

"And I don't mean your mom."

I called upon memories of grandmothers, aunts and anyone else who had innocently brushed my cheeks or even my lips with their own.

"And no other relatives either."

"Okay, no I haven't," I said. "Are you happy?"

"Yes and no, I guess."

"What do you mean by that?"

"Well, obviously I feel sorry for you that you've never kissed a girl. But I think it'd be cool if I was your first. You wanna, Wheeler? Otherwise the first time you go in for the kiss, you're not going to know what the hell you're doing."

I scooted around in my seat so I was facing her,

and she draped her arm across the back of my neck. I know I must have looked shocked because I was. But who was I to argue with her logic?

"You wanna?" she repeated. I smelled mint on her breath.

How had I not noticed until that moment she wore her hair loose that night? That her sweater was tight? That her eyes shone from the interior light? That her cheeks (and mine) were flushed from the almost suffocating warmth blowing through the heater vents. She leaned towards me slightly, and like the gravitational pull of the sun I was sucked into her orbit, my lips blending with hers. Soft. Warm. Greeting her tongue with my own. Gathering the silky thickness of her sleek, glossy hair into my closed fist. How did I know what the hell I was doing? It felt so easy and . . . natural.

When it was over, and it was eventually over, I thought there'd be hell to pay. She pulled back, floating away from me like a helium balloon getting smaller and smaller until it finally disappears from sight. And only then did I see Fritzy again.

"Was that gross?" she asked in an uncharacteristically timid way.

"Definitely not gross," I said. "Weird maybe, but not gross."

"Was it like brother and sister?" She trailed her fingertips lightly across her lips as if searching for a remnant of the kiss.

"I don't know any brothers and sisters who do

that."

All sorts of appropriate wisecracks escaped me at the moment. Wisecracks that Gus would have easily come up with.

"It's okay though. We're still friends and it was a friendly thing, right?"

"Very friendly."

It, for sure, had been Heaven to me.

HAVE YOU EVER LOST SOMETHING . . .

. . . and spent hours searching for it only to have its location revealed to you by your subconscious when you were least expecting it? If you have, then you'll know exactly how plan B came to me.

It was late that night, long after I'd finally given up on everything that could be postponed until the next day. I laid in bed not really asleep but not really awake either. Fritzy was *on* my mind for blowing my mind.

We're still friends, she had said.

Did she really have the ability to compartmentalize like that? Did I? The kiss was nothing more than a grain of rice in the bowl that was the entirety of our friendship. And yet what a grain it was. One that flavored the bowl with such a pungent spice, it was impossible to ignore.

I played out the day in the movie of my mind searching for clues as to what prompted the kiss. Was our friendship now in jeopardy? Was there a deeper motive, or should I take it for what she said it was, an act of kindness to help me become a man? There was the phone call in the afternoon. The report of Pirkle prancing about in his tighty-whities. The recent visits to her house where I'd been granted rare access to her bedroom. I pushed the rewind button, and it stopped at the place where I walked into her house that day. Where I dropped my keys in the metal bowl on the entry table. I rewound it again and pressed pause. I grabbed my phone.

"Wheeler," came her sleepy voice.

"Did I wake you?"

"Yeah . . . what's going on?"

"When Scolari comes to your house . . . does he put his keys in the brass bowl?"

Silence.

"I'm not sure. Maybe. Everyone usually does."

"Plan B," I said. "Next time he comes, you take his keys and let me inside his house. Then you go home and put them back in the bowl."

"You know what you're saying is completely insane, don't you?"

I thought about it for two seconds.

"Yeah. It's completely insane."

"What if he has a burglar alarm?"

"We run."

"Great plan, Wheeler."

"I don't remember seeing a burglar alarm sign out front or on the windows. Usually people do that if they have an alarm. But I can double check."

"That's called breaking and entering, and it's a felony. You're eighteen. You'd go to jail. I probably would too."

"Well, technically it's just entering. Not breaking because we're using his key. No one will ever know, and I'll be in and out in less than two minutes."

"What if he has hidden cameras in his house?"

"He's a piano teacher, Fritzy, not a computer geek."

"Wheeler?"

"Yeah?"

"This is so fucked up I can't even talk about it anymore. And it's totally not you. In fact, I'm wondering right now if you're on something."

"Think about it."

"I gotta go back to sleep. Bye."

"Bye."

Had the kiss somehow made me feel invincible? Had it scrambled my brains?

>>>

The following morning I saw it for the crazy plan that it was, and I probably would have dismissed it completely if three consecutive events hadn't occurred shortly thereafter.

Event number one happened when I stopped by Mrs. Dickinson's to pick up Lady.

"Hudson, dear," Mrs. Dickinson said. "A word, if you don't mind."

Of course, The Boys did mind. Lady too. They knew their routine and didn't appreciate any deviations from it. But when Jennifer struck a show dog pose, the others seemed to understand they must summon their better, more patient, selves. Felix teetered cautiously on his three legs before lowering himself to the carpet until further notice. Buster perched at Felix's side, and Lady was content to gaze adoringly at her handsome Prince Jennifer.

"I saw Len Pirkle the other day," Mrs. Dickinson said. "He stopped by the Senior Center, and of course I haven't seen him for a good long while. But his appearance was . . . disheveled, if I can be so blunt. I wonder if you would mind sharing your recent impressions. He *is* still your client, isn't he?"

"Yes, he is." I squirmed inside. I knew she was expecting a good, long talk about the whole thing. She wasn't the kind of woman who happily took "no" for an answer, and she was my number one client, after all. "But I can't speak about my other clients, I hope you understand. Privacy issues."

She looked me up and down and pursed her lips thoughtfully. The artist in me noticed the color of her lipstick, just a shade or two darker than her fingernails, but still complementary.

"No, I suppose you can't," she said at last.

But her look was clear. *He's your client so do something about it.*

Event number two happened the following day when Pirkle called to see if I could stop by.

"If you're coming out this way to visit your lady friend," he added.

I hadn't planned on it. In fact, I was planning to avoid Fritzy for a few days and let the dust settle, considering how dusty things had become. But he was asking, so I went.

"Have you been over there?" Pirkle asked. "To the neighbor's house."

I never felt comfortable in the living room where we were sitting just then. The neatness of it, the clean but sparse furnishings. It reminded me of one of those fake rooms they set up in a furniture store, unworthy of its name, the *living* room. I almost preferred the day it was vandalized. At least then it showed signs of life.

"Fritzy's?"

For a crazy second I thought he knew all about the kiss since that was still foremost on my mind.

"The character who lives behind me," he clarified with mild annoyance. "The one with the round window . . . the little girl."

I swallowed my words before I could blurt out the fact that we'd gone over there but been turned away at the door. I almost said it, I was so eager to report that I'd taken some action on his behalf. But I remembered Fritzy's warning about feeding into his paranoia.

"I haven't had a chance yet," I lied. "But I'll do it

soon, and when I do, I'll call you from the window."

"Good," he said, nodding his head. "That's why I called you. I'd like it if you could do that for me soon."

Mrs. Dickinson was right. He was looking a little disheveled. And it was very unlike him.

"Mr. Pirkle, do you wanna go somewhere?"

He looked surprised. "A particular place?"

"Not really," I said. "I just thought it might be nice to go for a walk. Or to get a cup of coffee or something."

I really wanted out of that house. It reminded me of all kinds of broken things. Furniture. Memories. Promises. Lives.

"I can offer you a cup of coffee," he gave me the skull-searching look which was comforting because it meant he was present. "But if you'd like to go out, then let's just walk down the street a-ways. There's a coffee shop about a quarter mile down. My treat."

Anyone who saw us walking would have taken us for grandfather and grandson. A very tall grandfather with his very short grandson. It felt good walking with him. I already had a grandfather, two in fact. But the one who was the father of my dad—him, I rarely saw. In my mind, he was the sad man who lived a long plane ride away. Our grip on each other had loosened over the years until it felt like it was almost gone.

Something about Pirkle reminded me of that grandfather before he got sad. And something else about Pirkle reminded me of that grandfather's son, my dad.

"How did you wind up here, sir? In this town."

The houses were newer where we were. On my side of town, the houses were old and small with more mature trees but no such thing as sidewalks or even streetlamps.

"I was born here. Grew up here. It looked a lot different back then. Nothing but walnut orchards and grazing cows for as far as the eye could see."

"I can't imagine that," I said, and I couldn't even though I tried to turn asphalt into pastures and sidewalks into walnut groves.

A tiny white dog that couldn't have weighed more than five pounds strained against its leash, dragging its heavyset owner faster than seemed possible. The dog stopped abruptly to sniff the tire of a parked car. The man pulled a phone from his pocket and poked at the screen before holding it up to his ear.

"You've heard of the one-room schoolhouse? Well I went to one. All the way from kindergarten to high school."

"So . . . Chuck lived here too?"

"We grew up about a hundred yards from each other. Not too far from here. Of course, none of these houses were here back then."

Somewhere behind us a car came to a sudden and unexpected stop. The screeching brakes startled Mr. Pirkle. We turned around but saw nothing.

"Must be over that way." I pointed in the direction of a busier parallel street.

"I'm getting worse, Hudson. I know I am."

"Have you seen her again?" I asked.

He nodded.

"Your mother . . . does she know things? I mean, if it comes to that."

It was my turn to nod.

"My mom's really smart. And she's a great nurse. She'll help you with anything."

"If it comes to that," he repeated. "I'm not so sure it will though. It depends which goes first, my brain or my body."

"You seem really healthy to me, sir."

"You mean physically? I suppose I am, but don't forget I'm ninety. People don't live forever, you know."

And at that moment I understood he was rooting for his body to give out. In the war between mind and body, he only wanted his sanity to last long enough to see him through the rest of his life.

"I've built a lot of walls, Hudson, and now I feel them crumbling down. Peeling away like the skin of an onion. Sometimes it seems I'm traveling back in time to the places I've spent my whole adult life trying to avoid."

"Did you have a happy childhood?"

We'd reached the coffee shop. It was one of those chain franchises filled, at that time of day, with young mothers and their preschool age children.

"What could be unhappy about a childhood when you have a best friend and a doting mother? I lost my father too, Hudson. Did I ever tell you that?"

He hadn't. With unspoken agreement, we turned back towards his house, leaving behind the steaming lattes unordered, unbought, and undrunk.

"How did he die?" I asked.

"He breathed in too much of that gas they used in the First World War. Mustard gas. Suffered from bad lungs for the rest of his life. I never had any brothers or sisters. My mother always said it was a miracle I was conceived."

I thought I could see the years slowly draining away, leaving him back in time when he was a teenager like me again. And then one day he'd go so far back all traces of him would disappear. I knew I'd be left with regrets if I let him go off by himself, with no one to mark that time for him. Someone had to remember.

"Remember," he said when I finally got in my car to leave, and for a second I thought he was talking about his life. But he wasn't, of course. He was only talking about the girl in the window.

Event number three began later that night.

It was the time of night which I like to think of as my reward for completing another day and hopefully doing it well. Achievements or enjoyments, anything beyond just marking time. My reward could be playing a video game, or reading a book, or even just lying in bed daydreaming which usually led to nightdreaming. The point was that nothing had a claim on me then. Nothing beyond my own desires.

That night I laid on my bed thinking about

Fritzy's kiss, wondering what Alana would think if she knew, wondering if I could somehow cause her to know—let it slip accidentally on purpose. I thought about Bryce who worried about losing Alana but skipped doing the easy things that would make her happy.

How this muddled brew of subconscious meanderings led to what came next, I'm not really sure. But somehow, on legs that didn't seem to be my own, I walked to my desk, and with similarly disconnected hands, I picked up my pencils and sketch pad and began to draw. Soon, words fell into place. Perfect words. And for the next four hours I didn't move from that spot. When I finally stopped to review what I'd done, it was like I was seeing it for the first time. *Ghost Soldiers*, I wrote without hesitation in bold block letters across the top of the page.

There were five ghost soldiers, all Americans. The young father killed by a roadside bomb in Iraq. The high school dropout from West Virginia, drafted and sent to fight and die in the jungles of Vietnam. The marine who lost both legs and his life on the bare rock of Iwo Jima. The wheezing, gasping WWI vet who made it back home only to succumb to the ravages of mustard gas. The teenage boy conscripted to fight in the Civil War after all the grown men had already been called up—dead from diphtheria and a hundred miles from home.

The ghost soldiers move together as a band of brothers, traveling backwards and forward through time to fight and die again and again in each other's wars. Young and old men battling ghosts and their own demons. Fighting alongside their brother ghosts. Every battle deepens their compassion. Deepens their understanding of the forces that dragged them into wars not of their own choosing. They watch over their loved ones from the spirit world. They relive their greatest sorrows and happiness, strengthened and supported by that brotherhood of five. They succeed in finding the humanity in their enemy. In themselves.

The characters were in the earliest stage of development. I knew I'd get to know them and absorb their worlds as my own. That could be months into the future. Maybe even years. But it felt important. It felt worthy, not just of me like Alana had said, but in a much broader context. Suddenly I felt a purpose to my life in a place that had previously been empty. It was more than just starting a business or impressing a girl or receiving a note from a teacher predicting I'd go places. Was it dark? Yes, very. But somehow it lightened me.

>>>

I floated through the next day and could hardly wait until that afternoon when Fritzy got home from a Christmas pageant rehearsal at her church. I was Superman on steroids. If a drug existed that could equal the high of a sense of purpose, we'd be a planet of junkies. I wanted to tell someone about it, and Alana was the natural person. But she was gone. Alana would have to wait.

In the meantime, plan B had taken on new meaning and urgency which only Fritzy could understand. But this time I wanted to talk to her about it face to face. It was too easy to dismiss it over the phone.

It turned out she was busy until after dinner, so as the sun set so did my faith in the plan. Only a few hours earlier I could have sold it to her or anyone else, believing in it with all my heart. I'd been so filled with self-assurance. Sitting with her in my car that night, I found it difficult to revive that conviction. But since we'd already discussed it once before, we were at least able to bypass the initial disbelief and charges of insanity. It wasn't as shocking this time although we were both a little scared by it, treating it carefully like a ticking bomb. But the longer we talked, the less scary it seemed. Like allergy shots where allergens are introduced little by little until one day the patient has become immune. Or the violence on TV that desensitizes against the real thing. And since the end result was for a moral purpose, it helped in justifying the means.

After a while, this plan—plan B—felt less like a bomb and more like a helpful pet. A guide dog that was going to lead us toward a solution to a problem that was hurting a very good man. I think anyone could have arrived at that same place under similar circumstances. You only need to believe you're acting in the name of righteousness. And that there is no other way.

Before setting the plan in motion, we had to eliminate all other options, so I attempted another visit to Mr. Scolari, this time by myself. I stopped by his house a few nights later around nine at night, a time Fritzy and I concluded a home burglar alarm would be enabled. It was Christmas Eve so I knew he'd be home. Alana would be back in three days. Plan B would take place in four. I did a quick check of the premises, saw no outside alarm signs and waited for him to answer my knock on his door.

He came quickly and, it seemed to me, without any indication that he had to first disable an alarm.

"Hudson."

I knew I was taking a big risk but I had to try. Fritzy insisted on it or she was out.

"Mr. Scolari, could I ask you for a huge favor?"

"What's this about?" he asked and I could tell he was annoyed.

The electric blue tones of a TV flickered behind him like a lightning storm.

"I wondered if I could take a look at your piano. I've been calling around to all the rental companies, and I want to make sure I get the right kind."

"Now?" he said with disbelief. "Any standard upright piano will do for a beginner." His body blocked the crack in the doorway. "You don't need to see mine, it's a baby grand which is totally unnecessary for you at this point."

It's a good thing it was dark because the anonymity of the night gave me that little extra courage it took to do something so stupid. What I was hoping for was to be invited in, and get to talking and then after a while I'd ask where the bathroom was and accidentally wander upstairs and call Pirkle from the window.

"Anyway, it's pretty late Hudson. Good to see you."

"Merry Christmas," I said while he closed the door on my face.

I knew I'd never get another chance. Not while he was home.

I walked back around to Pirkle's house and told him nobody was home. I'd have to try another time.

"I think you're wrong, Hudson," he said. "I just saw the little girl and this time she saw me too."

It was late and getting cold. My mother was expecting me home. Brightly colored lights trimmed the outside of Fritzy's house. The trees and bushes of one neighbor's front yard had been transformed into a light show of electric greens and blues. A twinkling tree was centered in the front window of the house next to that one. The sky was black and speckled with glittering stars. All around me the Christmas spirit seemed to mock the rabbit hole of Pirkle's mind.

"Merry Christmas, sir," I said.

>>>

Three days later came the call I'd been waiting for.

"I'm back," Alana said. "Totally jetlagged, but I really want to see you."

"I want to see you too. Did you have a good time?"

"It was amazing. But I missed you. Can you come over?"

She'd never invited me inside her house before. We always hung out at my house which she considered more fun and relaxing. Did absence really make the heart grow fonder? Would it work for me and not for Bryce? Was I going to get her father's blessing that night? I was just about to sit down for dinner with my mom but I was too anxious to get answers to those questions.

"I'm going to eat later," I told my mom. "Alana just got back from Paris."

My mom's shoulders rose and fell as she sighed visibly, not audibly. She knew enough not to say anything. "Cover your plate and put it in the fridge," she said wearily.

Once I got to Alana's, she threw open her door and hugged me tightly like a long, lost . . . brother?

"My dad's not home," she said as if to put me at my ease. It actually had the opposite effect. "He went straight to his office to catch up on work."

So much for her father's blessing.

Her house was a lot different than mine. For one thing, it was expensively and tastefully furnished and decorated. No threadbare sofas you could sink into for an afternoon nap like at my house. Her kitchen was all granite, stainless steel, and recessed lighting.

No stained Formica counters and buzzing fluorescent lights. No teachers' notes stuck to her massive refrigerator. My mom would have loved a kitchen like that, but we couldn't afford it.

"Nice digs, Alana."

Suddenly I felt an imbalance in our relationship I'd never felt before. Why hadn't I ever been invited to her house? Why had Bryce? What was different about now?

"Thanks. My dad always lets me decorate whenever we move. He gives me a budget and I can pretty much do whatever I want."

"You did all this?"

She led me into the living room. Like Pirkle's it didn't look too lived in, but it was beautiful. A curved buttery-soft leather sofa faced a huge flat screen TV. I could only imagine the hours I could waste playing video games if I lived there. Original artwork adorned the walls, and colorful glass sculptures were displayed in small alcoves.

"Mostly," she said. "A lot of the art my dad and I collected during our travels."

"Beautiful," I examined, without touching, a glass vase that seemed to change from blue to green to gold depending on where you stood, and how the light struck it.

"You'll be able to collect art pieces once you start traveling, Hudson."

"Doubt if I'll be able to afford anything like this."

She took me by the hand and led me up the stairs

to her bedroom.

"This is the room I reserve for the greatest art," she said.

Bryce wasn't lying. There were pictures of mine all over her walls. Sketches she'd saved from certain destruction.

Let me have it, she complained whenever I ripped a drawing from my pad in frustration. *You'll be famous one day, and then I'll be rich.*

I was beyond flattered.

"I can't wait for you to see my new graphic novel," I said. "I started it while you were gone, and this time I think you'll approve."

She looked at me with such delight and approval, I felt capable of anything. She seemed different. Happy. For whatever reason, the trip had been good for her.

"That's fantastic," she said. "I'm so proud of you." But she didn't ask when she could see it.

She took my hand in her own. Her fingers were soft and warm.

"I really did miss you, Hudson."

"You were only gone for eight days," I said.

Her sudden emotion was amazing, incredible, awesome—every superlative I could think of. But it also made me uncomfortable. My feelings for Alana never changed, so I wasn't sure what was behind the change in hers.

"Didn't you miss me?" she turned her pretty lips down to mimic a pout.

"You know I did." My vision went fuzzy with desire for her.

She sat on the side of her bed, pulling me next to her.

"How much?"

Was she really flirting with me? It *seemed* like she was, but since it was so far out of the realm of anything in our past, I decided it was just wishful thinking on my part.

"A lot," I said, and the memory of Fritzy's kiss pinged my brain.

I felt the hairs on the back of my neck stiffen like they say happens just before lightning strikes. Alana lowered herself onto her back and pulled me towards her. The flowering vine running down the side of her neck gave off an intoxicating aroma. Since she was experienced, I followed her lead, and suddenly the body I'd only ever dreamed of was open to me—to touch, to smell, to taste. A gasp. Her fluttering eyelashes. The kiss. Clothes peeling away. Flesh pressing against flesh. Melting into each other. It was the fourth of July, Christmas, and my birthday all rolled into one. Inside of a dream. And then just like a dream, it was over, and I woke up as the new Hudson. Hudson, the man. Hudson who wasn't a virgin. It was everything I'd ever fantasized about. And more.

Afterwards, we lay naked under her mauve satin comforter giggling like kids. She smiled at me in a way people do when they're wondering what's on your mind. But it wasn't my mind she was wondering about. It was hers. I feared a Fritzy-type question.

Please, God, don't let her say it, I prayed ungratefully to the God I only call on in times of distress. *Don't let her turn to me and ask if it was gross.*

She didn't. I summoned my courage.

"Are you really done with Bryce?"

"Of course I am." She stretched forward to kiss me on the lips. "We'll be great traveling partners, Hudson," she said.

And it was only then that I got it. I'd just passed my audition.

I'd become a man, which gave me the courage to go through with plan B. I didn't kid myself that Alana had gone to Paris for eight days and fallen out of love with Bryce and in love with me. I knew she just wanted to see if I passed. Not in terms of my love-making skills which were non-existent. Just in terms of the *"gross"* factor. Could she be with me, make love to me and not go running for the hills? Alana needed me to help her through the first part of life after parents. She didn't need me the way I needed her, but she was smart enough to know there'd come a time when just being friends wouldn't be enough for me. That's what she wanted to preempt.

Did I realize all that at the moment? Not exactly in a way I could put into words, but I knew it in my gut. It didn't matter to me. Not at the time.

WHEN GOOD IDEAS GO BADLY . . .

. . . maybe you have to go back and ask yourself if the idea was really good to begin with.

Fritzy and I were ready. We'd prepped and gone over contingencies. She noticed my new confidence, almost arrogance, but put it down to the fact I was psyched about what we were about to do. The act itself was taking on greater significance than the reason behind it.

I stopped by Pirkle's house just before Scolari arrived for Frankie's lesson.

"I'm on my way to your neighbor's house," I said. "When I get there, I'll look out the round window and call you on your cell phone."

"You didn't tell him anything?" Pirkle asked warily. He lived with the fear that any random person aware of his "problem" had the power to commit him to an asylum. Maybe back in the day they did, and nothing would convince him otherwise.

"No. I just said I'd stop by. There's a bathroom upstairs, so I'll tell him I have to use it."

He gazed steadily at me and nodded.

"I'll be waiting for your call."

How easily I'd learned to lie.

>>>

We were standing in the kitchen so I could see when Scolari arrived at Fritzy's, but she texted me anyway, and Plan B was set into motion. I left Pirkle's house and walked around the block to Scolari's street. I waited on the corner until Fritzy arrived.

"Can't believe we're doing this, Wheeler. This is so wrong." She was breathing heavily even though she'd barely exerted herself.

"Not a good time for cold feet," I said. "C'mon, we can do this. In and out in less than three minutes. No one will ever know I was there."

"Remember, don't touch *anything. Anything!*"

"I won't. Relax. Let's go."

We jogged the rest of the way to his house and after looking around to make sure there were no passersby or curious neighbors, we walked to the front door. Fritzy tried a few different keys before finding the one that unlocked the door. She turned it carefully, and we held our breath, hoping an alarm wouldn't go off. It didn't. Then just as she turned to leave, we proved the old proverb that the best laid plans often go wrong. And ours wasn't even the best laid.

"Shit," Fritzy said. "How are you going to lock the door when you leave if I take the keys back with me?"

It was a deadbolt, so I couldn't lock it from the inside and pull it shut behind me like we'd planned.

"Too risky to give me the keys. Just take them. I'll pull the door shut and when he unlocks it, hopefully he won't notice anything. If he notices, maybe he'll think he forgot to lock up. Now get out. Go home."

I slipped inside and closed the door quietly behind me. I surveyed the darkened room, curtains drawn against the light of day. I could make out a beautiful baby grand piano in a room obviously meant to be the dining room. I moved towards it and ran my fingers against its glossy black surface before remembering the fingerprint evidence I might be leaving behind. Too late to worry about that. I was the star of my own crime show, and Fritzy was going to want every last detail. I looked around, saw the stairs, and walked towards them.

Later I'd learn that Fritzy ran all the way home probably getting there soon after I reached the stairs. She didn't hear the plinking of piano keys when she walked into her house. Instead she heard the murmuring of voices. Voices coming towards her. She quickly dropped the keys into the brass bowl.

"You'd better go see Mom," Frankie said as he and Scolari walked towards the front door. "She's in her room crying. The hospital just called and said

Grandpa died."

"I'm so sorry, Lauren." Mr. Scolari put a gentle hand on Fritzy's shoulder. I imagined him reaching up to do it when Fritzy later described it to me. "Frankie, you take care, and I'll see you next week unless you let me know otherwise."

He reached into the bowl for the keys and walked out of their house.

>>>

When Fritzy called me I was halfway up the stairs.

"Get out!" she hissed into the phone. "Scolari's on his way home. My grandpa died, so they canceled the lesson."

"I'm almost there," I said. "When did he leave?"

"Just now. Get out. I mean it, Wheeler. I have to go help my mom; she's really upset."

I took "just now" to mean *just now*, but it really didn't. There had been the seconds ticking away when Fritzy peeked into her mother's bedroom. When she walked to her own room, shutting the door against Frankie's helpless gaze in order to call me. There had been the seconds when she listened to make sure Frankie was in the room with their mom. Seconds. Everything we do in life strips away the seconds we have left. Even the little things we never think about. I thought I had a minute to get up the stairs and call Mr. Pirkle. It would take Scolari five to seven minutes to walk home. He wouldn't be running like Fritzy. I double-stepped it to the top of the stairs, as fast as my legs could carry me. The window, by my calculation, was only a few feet away. My lungs were burning by the time I reached the second story. My heart was pounding and my skin and scalp prickling with primal fear. My eyes swept up and down the hallway. There it was. The round window I'd seen so many times from the other side, it almost seemed mythical. I started towards it, cell phone in hand, Pirkle's number already ringing.

And then she stepped out of a room. A little girl with curly blonde hair. She looked at me fearfully but quickly composed herself.

"Shhh . . . don't tell Mommy." She brought a tiny finger up to her lips.

WHEN BAD IDEAS GO WELL...

. . . you should never expect to get credit.

What went through my mind at that moment will never be recovered. Only when I think back can I try to piece it together. The girl. My total inability to process her existence. My completely inappropriate laughter at the realization the joke was on me. Joke? 911? What was that signal I was supposed to give Pirkle from the window? What signal should I use for a real girl? What the hell was going on? I grabbed her by the hand and walked quickly to the stairs. Why? I have no idea. Where was I taking her? I don't know that either. All I knew was that she wasn't supposed to be there, and that's what I had to change. *Don't tell Mommy*. I won't. Come with me. Who is Mommy? Who is Daddy? Everything unfolded like a bad dream. One where you pray for the alarm clock to wake you up.

Scolari arrived on the wings of all those precious seconds. The ones that didn't exist for me but were real for him. He did notice the unlocked door. Of course he did. He wasn't operating on automatic the way I was. He wasn't moving through a dream. He was always thinking first and foremost of the little girl in his house. The one he thought he was protecting. The one I guess he really *was* protecting. An unlocked door, well that was a red alert at the highest level. He burst into the house not even taking the time to close the door behind him. I was almost down the stairs by then, standing on the last step with the girl's tiny hand still clutched in my own. And then, as if in slow motion, I saw the lights come on. I heard him call out her name.

"Stella!"

I'll never forget that name for as long as I live. *Stella.*

When he saw us frozen on that last step, he went ballistic. He charged towards me, I believe ready to kill. Like that deer in the headlights, I found it impossible to move. I found it impossible to speak. Then I released Stella's hand and took the final step to face what was coming next.

"You son-of-a-bitch!" was the last thing I heard him say before he swung his fist, catching me square on the jaw. I fell backwards and heard Stella scream.

There was something hard on the back of my tongue. It was my tooth. I tasted blood. Lots of it. He swung again and again. His left hand held me down by my throat while his right fist made hamburger out of my face.

"Son-of-a-bitch," he said over and over again with each punch.

I felt myself losing consciousness. I struggled to focus on something, anything. Even his fist. I coughed hard on the tooth that was making its way down my throat.

I heard her before I saw her. To my rattled brain she looked every inch the avenging angel, complete with an aura of light. "Stop!" Fritzy's commanding voice yanked me back into the world. "Stop it!" she screamed as she grabbed for the arm that was preparing to take yet another swing. Scolari was no match for her power. She pulled him off of me and put up her fists, ready to fight. I focused on my angel through the slits that had become my eyes.

"It's not his fault," she said. "We were just trying to help someone. An old man."

I could hear Stella crying hysterically.

"Now look what you've done," Scolari's voice cracked. "Look what you've done. Come here, baby." He leaned over and Stella ran down the remaining steps and into his arms, burying her face in his chest

I pushed myself up onto my elbows. The room was spinning. I saw Fritzy. I saw Scolari with Stella wrapped in his arms. I saw his bleeding knuckles and worried whether he'd ever be able to play the piano again. As for myself, I was beyond pain. I couldn't feel a thing.

"He won't tell Mommy," Stella sobbed. "He's nice, Daddy. He said he won't tell."

"Shhh, baby, shhh. It's okay, honey."

I tried to sit up but fell back down on my elbows. Fritzy stood guard, waiting for Scolari's next move.

And then just like in the movies, Pirkle walked through the open front door.

"Mr. Pirkle," Scolari said. "What the hell are you doing here? What are you *all* doing here?"

"This your little girl?" Pirkle asked as he walked past Scolari and knelt down by my side. "Come on, Hudson. You're going to be all right, buddy. I got you."

He lifted me into his arms and took my entire weight until I was as steady as I was going to be. Then he walked me slowly towards the door. Fritzy came up behind us and took my other arm.

"She's my daughter," Scolari said. "Her mother . . . she's unfit. No child should have to go through that." Scolari's voice was raw with emotion.

"Better sort it out with the judge," Pirkle said without even turning around.

"You don't know what you're doing. You don't know what her mother's like. I'm trying to *save* her."

Pirkle stopped in his tracks just as we reached the door. He turned around and gave Scolari *the look*.

"How do you save someone by making them disappear?" he asked.

Pirkle was right. He should know. He'd made

himself disappear for most of his life.

>>>

Lucky for me, my mom was a nurse so I got to recuperate at home. Luckier still I was home-schooled because I would have missed a whole lot of school otherwise.

Alana came to see me and burst into tears. She left five minutes later. She came a few days later and burst into tears again. She managed to stay ten minutes that time. It was too painful for her to see me in all that pain. To be fair, I felt like bursting into tears every time I looked in the mirror.

Fritzy came to see me every day. Sometimes we just watched TV and sometimes we talked about what had happened. She gave me a hard time for being lazy and told me it was going to take her an extra six months just to get me back into running shape, but she supposed it could be done. She took over my Distress Dial duties, and Frankie took care of walking the dogs. At first her parents forbade her from seeing me, but she told them they could do whatever they wanted to her, but she was going to keep on being my friend no matter what. They let it go, saying that loyalty was probably a more admirable quality than a good choice in friends.

As for my mom, I knew how much I'd disappointed her.

"I can't very well ground you now that you're eighteen. And I suppose you've been punished enough.

There's nothing I can do to cure stupid, so hopefully you'll use better judgment in the future."

I used the time to work on *Ghost Soldiers,* which I still hadn't shown anyone. One day I heard my mom sniffling from my bedroom where she was changing the sheets. The sniffling kept coming at regular intervals until it became obvious it was more than her hay fever. I went to my room where I found her sitting on the side of my bed, my manuscript on her lap.

"I remember the toy car," she looked up at me when I walked in. "But I didn't know you remembered it too."

I sat down beside her and took her hand in mine. She leaned against my shoulder and wept quietly.

"I don't know what I'd do without you, Hudson. You're my boy. You're my life."

I cried for the first time since I'd traded my regular eyes for puffy, black and blue slits.

>>>

One Saturday the doorbell rang and my mom led Mr. Pirkle to my room.

"How you doing, son?" he asked. "You're not looking too shabby." He turned to my mom. "That's one tough customer," he said, and she smiled.

"How did you know Scolari?" That question had been haunting me ever since I heard Scolari call Pirkle by name.

"Once had a conversation with him at the coffee shop," he said. "Didn't remember his name. I'd see him at your lady friend's house from time to time, but I had no idea he was my backyard neighbor."

"Why did you go to his house?"

"You dialed my phone. I could hear everything that was going on."

My mother looked visibly upset, excused herself and left the room.

"I've come from the doctor," he told me in a hushed tone. "Just like we agreed."

"But you were right. There *was* a girl in the window."

"Well, I was right, but I was wrong too. You paid a big price for me, and I owed it to you. And to myself."

"What did he say?"

"*She* said I'd do better in one of those places where there are people around who could keep an eye on me. Your mother was right. 'Sundowners' is what the doctor called it."

"So, what are you going to do?"

"I got some names of places from your friend, Mrs. Dickinson, who, by the way, sends her best wishes. I suppose I'll check out a few of them."

"You want me to go with you? As soon as I'm feeling a little better?"

"I'd like nothing more." He ran his hand over his thick silver hair. "It took a lot of courage, Hudson. What you did for me."

But I knew I wasn't brave. I never expected what happened.

And Mr. Scolari who wasn't really Mr. Scolari.

He was Noel Albertsen who moved to our town two years prior when he rented the house in preparation for taking his daughter from the woman who was failing her, the drug-addicted mother. The courts repeatedly ignored the problem or at least overlooked it, but Noel Albertsen couldn't. Fritzy's mom had first seen his name on the bulletin board of a local music store. The fact that he came to his students' homes was a big plus for her and many others.

Can you kidnap your own child? Apparently. Can you ignore a law for good reason, or break a law that's unjust? You can, but you have to accept the consequences. He did. I did. But he didn't press charges against me, and I didn't press charges against him either. In that way, we saved each other from even worse trouble than we'd already found. Over the next few months there were stories about him on the local news. Noel Albertson was sent to prison, and Stella was put into temporary foster care. A few months later he was released and Stella was returned to his custody when the judge determined the father was only looking out for his child's best interests and had been forced into a no-win situation. Noel and Stella Albertson moved away to begin a new life. Did the system finally work? I guess it did.

>>>

Instead of growing closer, Alana and I began to drift after the night we made love. When I finally did get around to showing her the manuscript and drawings for *Ghost Soldier*, she was filled with praise. She finally gave me the validation I craved from her, but once I got it, I realized I no longer needed it. I found the reward in my work, and I found it all by myself. And there was something else I discovered. I didn't really want to travel to Europe. I just wanted Alana.

Alana and I made plans to go to the all-night party the night of our high school graduation. But that afternoon she called to say she couldn't do it. Being in the school gym, (which had been transformed to look like Las Vegas) with Bryce and his friends for an entire night was way too depressing. Two days later she texted to say she'd be spending a few weeks with her mom and sister. I never saw her again. Three months later, her father was transferred to another city and their house was for sale.

Alana Love had been disappointed early in life and seemed to seek out disappointment to confirm her world view. But beyond that, she was like a sweet summer breeze. Irresistible as it flows over you. Caresses you. But you can never latch on.

GOING PLACES...

Pirkle moved into an assisted living home where he lived independently with just the right level of support. One day a *For Sale* sign grinned like a fang from his front lawn. Eventually the sign disappeared, and a young family moved in. One day I saw them all piling into the van in the driveway—the parents and their two children, a small boy and his blonde, curly-haired younger sister.

Pirkle wasn't a Distress Dial client anymore. I never got another late-night phone call from him. We started over as friends, but maybe that's what we were all along in our own way. I visited him nearly every day. And then early one morning, because I was his emergency contact, I got a call from the director of the assisted living facility where Pirkle lived. He'd passed away comfortably in his sleep. At last, he was at peace.

My mother and Fritzy went with me to collect his belongings. The director gave me a small box.

"He specifically said that nobody should open this except for you, Hudson. He said it was the only valuable thing he had to pass along."

With trembling hands, I opened it under the watchful eyes of my mother and Fritzy. It was a small metal star suspended on a blue ribbon. At the time, I knew nothing about the Medal of Honor. There was also a letter addressed to me, intended for my eyes only after he was gone. I couldn't bring myself to read it, though. I wasn't ready. Not yet. Lastly, placed carefully at the bottom of the box was the frayed photograph of the little girl. Of *his* little girl. And suddenly, I knew what I needed to do.

>>>

Fritzy and I planned a road trip right after graduation. Roundtrip, it was a distance of nearly two thousand miles. Our destination was Rock Springs, Wyoming—a small city where my internet sleuthing had finally led me to Pirkle's daughter.

There were few instances in my life when ringing a doorbell was such a heart-pounding event, but it seemed like they all had to do with Fritzy in one way or another. I thought about the time I rang her doorbell, awkwardly looking for a way to beg forgiveness for being such a bad sport during that first game of HORSE. Or the times I'd rung Scolari's bell looking for a way to get in. Fritzy squeezed my hand, and I took a deep breath.

When the door swung open, it was hard to connect the gray-haired old lady who stood before me to Maggie, the little girl in the picture I'd seen so often in Pirkle's home. I instantly recognized her father's eyes, the set of his mouth, his commanding presence—that much was plain. She had advance notice of our trip so we hadn't caught her off-guard, but maybe nothing can prepare you for a meeting like that. I was the grandson her father never had, although I knew Maggie had children, even grandchildren of her own. Would she hold that against me? I couldn't be sure.

She invited us into her neat but cozy family room.

"I'm a widow," she explained. "Lost my husband just two years ago, but it still feels like he's here. I'm always blurting out something or other to him."

Fritzy nodded her head seriously.

"I'm sorry for your loss," I said. It seemed like such a trite phrase. One I'd heard people say when they were powerless to match the moment.

"Can I get you something?" she asked, which brought a tight feeling in my throat. I remembered how Pirkle never let me spend more than a few minutes in his home without the offer of some type of drink.

"No thank you, ma'am," Fritzy said. "We stopped off for lunch before we got here."

"I know a little of why you're here," Maggie said. "From Hudson's email. But why are you *really* here?"

And for the first time in all those miles of traveling, I actually thought about the true answer to that question. Ostensibly, I knew why I was there. To offer the few possessions that Pirkle had left behind. But why was I really there? To capture a part of Pirkle which would allow me to hold onto him a little bit longer? Or was it the desire to solve the mystery of the little girl in the picture the way I'd solved the mystery of the girl in the window?

"He left behind a few things. I wanted you to have them." I reached into the small box I'd brought with me.

"Really?" She arched an eyebrow at me in just the same way Pirkle would have. "You could have mailed those and saved yourself a long trip."

"We wanted to—"

"I wanted to meet you," I interrupted. Fritzy was always tried to shield me, but this was something I had to answer myself. "He meant a lot to me . . . your father. He talked a lot about you." I held out the Medal of Honor.

Maggie extended her hand to take the medal. She turned it over and examined it for the precious thing it was. Her fingers closed around it. "I had a real father, you know. I don't want you kids feeling sorry for me. My birth father was . . . a complicated man, but I'm betting he left this for you."

"He did," Fritzy blurted out, and I nudged her thigh with my knee. "What?" she hissed under her breath.

"I had a real father," Maggie repeated. "A real father who always stood by me. I would never do anything to dishonor his memory. This was meant for you. You keep it. Now, what else you got in that box?"

I pulled out the tiny picture of the little girl, her hair a halo of ringlets. In a way, it was the hardest thing for me to surrender because it was Pirkle's most precious possession.

"There's this." I offered it to her, half-hoping she'd turn it down.

She stared at the photo as though meeting a long-lost daughter. A child given up for adoption only to be reunited many decades later.

"I'll keep this one," she said so quietly, I had to strain to hear her.

> > >

As Fritzy drove the first leg home, I sat in the passenger seat watching the rolling hills go by, and I finally felt ready. Reaching into the backseat, I unzipped the side pocket of my backpack and pulled out the crumpled white envelope. I traced my fingers over the cursive letters on the front. *For Hudson.* I carefully ripped open the flap, pulled out the hand-written letter, and read.

In the letter, Pirkle discussed his hope that I'd change my mind and go to college after all. He talked about other things too . . . Regrets . . . Blessings . . . The way a grandfather would talk to his grandson. He talked about a small fund he had set up in my name.

One that would help to pay for college if I decided to go, and would otherwise revert to me at the age of twenty-five. But it was the last sentence of his letter that froze my heart.

If ever there was a young man who was going places, it's you, Hudson.

I'd never told him about the note from my teacher, the one that taunted me from the refrigerator door, daring me to prove my worth to the world. It was an expectation I never wanted. Instead of filling me with confidence, it had the opposite effect and always made me feel inadequate. Was Mr. Pirkle's letter a new curse from the grave?

In the days that followed, I read the letter over and over until one morning I woke up and read it with brand new eyes. I suddenly understood that no matter what other people want or expect, only my expectations counted in the end. I realized that everyone was going places. Fritzy, me, my mom. Alana was going to places I'd never see. And Mr. Pirkle had been to Hell as a young man, but now I hoped he was in a better place, if there is such a thing.

And then something else hit me. I knew exactly where I was going. I was going to college. During one of our many talks after he sold his house, Mr. Pirkle told me that the most difficult thing a man has to do in life is to open his heart to someone. In his mind, he had failed, but I knew different. I knew he had succeeded. And I knew that one day I would too.

GHOST SOLDIERS
by Hudson Wheeler
(background notes)

Medal of Honor

-Established in 1861 by Abraham Lincoln

-Has been awarded to 3516 recipients since its inception

-The highest military honor for valor above and beyond the call of duty in action against an enemy force

-Illegal to sell

-Often awarded posthumously

-Entitles the recipient to a salute from all troops, even those who outrank him/her

-Entitles the recipient to a monthly stipend for life

Battle of Iwo Jima (WWII)

-Lasted 5 weeks

-70,000 American soldiers participated

-6800 Americans killed; 19,217 wounded

-Of the 22,000 original Japanese combatants, nearly all died either from fighting or by ritual suicide.

-Gave birth to one of the most memorable military photographs of all time, the raising of the flag over Mount Suribachi

Major US War Military Fatalities

-Civil War - 625,000

-World War I - 116,516 American military

-World War II - 405,399 American military

-Vietnam - 58,209 American military

-Afghanistan/Iraq - 6890+ (ongoing) American military

ACKNOWLEDGMENTS

First and foremost, thank you to George Berla, who keeps me writing through his expectations, love, and belief in me.

Thank you to Amberjack Publishing. Dayna, Kayla, Jenny, and Cami, I couldn't ask for a more hardworking or insightful group to have my back.

Many thanks to Jeremy, Lucas, Corey, and Samantha Berla, and Nishita for your love, support, feedback, glitch-fixing and general superior abilities.

This book is dedicated to the men and women of the armed forces who have sacrificed their lives or their peace of mind on behalf of us all; and to the belief that generations must reach out to each other over the decades that separate us, to capture and preserve the hopefulness of youth and the wisdom of age.

ABOUT THE AUTHOR

Kathryn Berla is the author of the young adult novels, *12 Hours in Paradise, Dream Me,* and *The House at 758.* She graduated from the University of California at Berkeley and currently resides in the San Francisco Bay Area.